BOOK 1

THE BOY WHO CRASHED TO EARTH

BY JUDD WINICK

WITH COLOUR BY GUY MAJOR

PUFFIN

PUFFIN BOOKS

UK | USA | Canada | Ireland | Australia | India | New Zealand | South Africa

Puffin Books is part of the Penguin Random House group of companies whose addresses can be found at global.penguinrandomhouse.com.

www.penguin.co.uk www.puffin.co.uk www.ladybird.co.uk

First published in the United States of America by Random House Children's Books, a division of Random House LLC, 2015
Published in Great Britain by Puffin Books 2017

001

Book design by John Sazaklis

Printed in China

A CIP catalogue record for this book is available from the British Library

ISBN: 978–0–141–37692–9

All correspondence to:
Puffin Books
Penguin Random House Children's
80 Strand, London WC2R 0RL

"Stayed in from recess to read it . . . **CAN'T WAIT FOR NEXT ONE!**"

—Zac, age 9

"*Hilo* was **SO GREAT** I couldn't stop reading until I'd finished it. I want to read the next one **NOW**!"

—Jack, age 10

"I love all the funny parts— it's just **'OUTSTANDING!'** And his **SILVER UNDERPANTS** are hilarious."

—Bennett, age 5

"I **LOVE** this book because it is **EXCITING** and **FUNNY.**"

—Nate, age 8

"My big brother and I fight over this book. **I CAN'T WAIT** for the second one so we can both read a Hilo book at the same time."

—Nory, age 8

"**FANTASTIC. EVERY SINGLE THING ABOUT THIS . . . IS TERRIFIC.**"

—Boingboing.net

"**HIGH ENERGY** and **HILARIOUS**!"

—Gene Luen Yang, winner of the Printz Award

"*Hilo* is **REALLY, REALLY FUNNY.** It has a **LOT OF LAUGHS.** The raccoon is the funniest. It made me feel really happy!"

—Theo, age 7

"**ACTION-PACKED** and **AMAZING FUN.**"

—Brad Meltzer, THE FIFTH ASSASSIN

"*Hilo* is loads of **SLAPSTICK FUN**!"

—Dan Santat, winner of the Caldecott Medal

HILO #1 THE BOY WHO CRASHED TO EARTH

HILO #2 SAVING THE WHOLE WIDE WORLD

HILO #3 THE GREAT BIG BOOM

FOR

the Catman and the tuff Little kitten

CHAPTER

AAAAAAH!

HELLO.

AAAH!!

MY NAME IS D. J.
AAAAAH!

AND THIS IS MY FRIEND HILO.
AAAAAAAH!

AND THIS IS WHEN WE MET.
AAAAAAHHHHH!!

IT WAS A **REALLY** WEIRD DAY.

AAAAHH!

AAAAAAA--
AAAAAAAAAAA

AAAAAAA--

AAAHH!!

OOF!
OOF!

POOF
POOF
CLICK
CLICK
SHUCK
SHUCK
SHUCK
TOONK
TOONK
AAH!
AAH!

BLAM

AAAAHH!!

SCRAAAAACCK

CHAPTER

GOOD AT ONE THING

MY NAME IS **DANIEL JACKSON LIM.** EVERYONE CALLS ME **D. J.**

AND I'M NOT GOOD AT ANYTHING.

I'M NOT SAYING THAT I'M A **TOTAL** DORK. THERE'S JUST NOTHING THAT I'M REALLY SUPER GOOD AT.

WHICH IS HARD IN MY FAMILY. THERE ARE **FIVE** OF US KIDS.
I HAVE TWO OLDER BROTHERS AND TWO YOUNGER SISTERS.
AND THEY ARE ALL **AWESOME** AT SOMETHING.

LOUIS PLAYS TENNIS.
17 YEARS OLD

DEXTER IS A WHIZ AT CHEMISTRY.
13 YEARS OLD

JENNIFER PLAYS VIOLIN. AND SINGS. **AND** DANCES BALLET.
9 YEARS OLD

AND LISA DOES **EVERYTHING** TWO YEARS EARLY. WALKING, TALKING, MATH, SWIMMING. SEVEN YEARS OLD AND ALREADY IN THE THIRD GRADE.

ME? I DON'T DO BETTER THAN OKAY IN EVERYTHING.
ME. 10 YEARS OLD.
EXCEPT **ONE** THING. THERE WAS JUST ONE THING I WAS GOOD AT.

GINA.
I WAS GOOD AT BEING FRIENDS WITH GINA.

SHE LIVED NEXT DOOR TO US SINCE I WAS TWO.
GINA!!
GIIIIINA!

CHECK IT OUT! **CHECK IT OUT!** MR. ANTONELLI HAD ANOTHER GARAGE SALE!
SERIOUSLY? HE HAS ONE EVERY WEEK. AND EVERYTHING SMELLS LIKE FEET.
YEAH, WELL, THIS IS **FOOT STINK FREE.** HE GAVE IT TO ME FOR A DOLLAR.

WHAT IS IT?
DON'T DIE. IT'S SO AWESOME, YOU MAY DIE.

WHAT IS IT?!

TUNK

AN ENTIRE BOX OF PLASTIC ELEPHANTS.

WHOA.
I KNOW.
WHOA.
I KNOW.

WHAT SHOULD WE DO WITH THEM?

FLYING ELEPHANTS!!

CLUB
House

IT WAS COOL.

THEN...
WHEN WE WERE SEVEN YEARS OLD...

HER DAD GOT A NEW JOB. AND THEY MOVED AWAY.
RUA 1712

I WAS FRIENDS WITH GINA AND I WAS GOOD AT THAT.

SHE LEFT AND I WASN'T GOOD AT ANYTHING.

THREE YEARS LATER

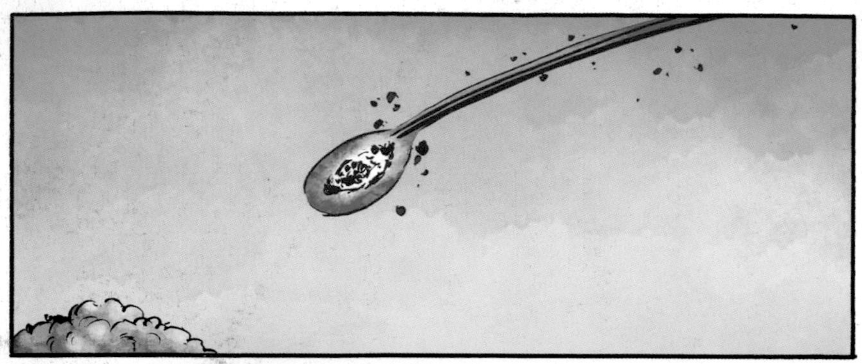

BOOM

HOLY MACKEREL.

CHAPTER

BOOM

WHOA.

OW.

WHOA!

UM, WHAT? I DON'T UNDERSTAND. DO YOU ... DO YOU NEED A HAND?

SNAP

OUCH.

HEY.
AAAAH!

AAAAH!

IS THAT A GREETING? I LIKE IT!
AAAAH!

WHERE AM I?
BERKE COUNTY.
NEVER HEARD OF IT.
WHO ARE YOU?

UM ... I'M **D. J.**
WHAT'S THIS GREEN STUFF, D. J.?

IT'S GRASS.
IT SMELLS OUTSTANDING!
WHO ARE YOU?
I DON'T REMEMBER. THAT COULD BE A PROBLEM.
MY MEMORY IS A BUSTED BOOK.
BUSTED BOOK?
YEP. MISSING A LOTTA PAGES. GAPS! HOLES!
FOR EXAMPLE, HOW DID I GET HERE?
ARE YOU KIDDING? IT WAS INSANE! YOU FELL FROM THE SKY!
I DID?
YEAH! YOU DON'T REMEMBER? MAYBE YOU HIT YOUR HEAD.
I FELL FROM THE SKY. I HIT EVERYTHING.

THIS TASTES TERRIBLE.
DON'T **EAT** THAT!

ARE YOU FROM OUTER SPACE OR SOMETHING?
MAYBE. THAT'D BE A GOOD GUESS.

YOU DON'T KNOW? WHAT'S WRONG WITH YOU?
I JUST FELL OUT OF THE SKY. THERE'S **LOTS** OF THINGS WRONG WITH ME.

YEAH. WELL -- **HEY!** WHERE ARE YOU GOING?

WHERE DO YOU LIVE?

OVER THERE.

OUTSTANDING! C'MON!

WHAT?! WAIT!
I'M COMING! WAIT!
WAIT!

YOU DROPPED
YOUR ELEPHANT!

WHAT?
SKIIIIIID

DOES IT TASTE OKAY?
OKAY? IT'S OUTSTANDING! WHAT IS IT?!
RICE.
OUTSTANDING!
AND WHAT IS THIS LIQUID?!
MILK.
OUTSTANDING!
YOU'VE NEVER EATEN RICE OR MILK BEFORE?
NOPE! I DON'T THINK I'VE EVER EATEN **ANYTHING** BEFORE.
HOW CAN YOU HAVE NEVER **EATEN** BEFORE?
YOU **TOTALLY** DON'T REMEMBER ANYTHING ABOUT, WELL, WHERE YOU'RE FROM?

NOPE! DON'T KNOW **WHERE** I'M FROM! **WHY** I'M HERE! **WHO** I AM! NOPE! NOPE! NOPE!
HA! MILK!
TUNK

BUT I FELL FROM THE SKY AND **NOW** I'M EATING RICE AND MILK! I FEEL PRETTY GOOD THAT THINGS WILL SORT THEMSELVES OUT.

MAYBE YOU'RE AN ALIEN OR A GOVERNMENT EXPERIMENT.
"GOVERNMENT EXPERIMENT"?
I DO **NOT** LIKE THE SOUND OF THAT.
Daniel
Daniel

WAIT ... HANG ON ...

WHAT?

BURP!
WHAT WAS THAT?!
YOU BURPED!
OUTSTANDING! I WANT TO DO THAT AGAIN!
YOU MIGHT HAVE TO WAIT A FEW MINUTES.
HERE.
THIS IS SOME OF MY OLD STUFF YOU COULD WEAR.
WHY? I'M COMFORTABLE. BREEZY.
MAN, YOU CAN'T GO AROUND NEARLY NAKED. YOU NEED TO BE SPORTING MORE THAN THOSE SILVER UNDERPANTS.
I LIKE THEM.
DUDE.
FINE.
HEY, THESE CLOTH WRAPS FEEL NICE.
THEY'RE CALLED CLOTHES.

SORRY, I'M DOING THE BEST I CAN WITH THE VOCABULARY I ABSORBED FROM YOU.

YOU **ABSORBED** MY VOCABULARY?

YEAH, WHEN WE TOUCHED HANDS.

HEY, WHERE DID --
THIS PLACE IS **BIG!**

DO YOU LIVE HERE BY YOURSELF?
NO, I LIVE WITH MY FAMILY. BUT THEY'RE OUT.
OUT?

MY DAD IS WORKING LATE. MY MOM IS AT MY AUNT HELEN'S. MY OLDER BROTHER IS AT TENNIS PRACTICE. MY **OTHER** BROTHER IS AT SCIENCE CLUB. MY LITTLE SISTER IS AT BALLET REHEARSAL. AND MY OTHER LITTLE SISTER IS AT A PIANO LESSON.

I DON'T DO ANYTHING. SO I'M HERE.

I WOULDN'T SAY YOU DON'T DO **ANYTHING.** I FELL FROM THE SKY AND YOU GAVE ME RICE AND MILK.

I THINK THAT'S COOLER THAN WHATEVER TENNIS PRACTICE IS.
SNIFF

BUT BALLET REHEARSAL SOUNDS NEAT.
CAN YOU EAT THESE? BECAUSE THEY SMELL **AWFUL.**

NO, THESE ARE SHOES. YOU WEAR --
HEY, WHAT ARE YOU DOING WITH THAT MARKER?
I DON'T KNOW.
IT JUST FEELS LIKE . . .
FEELS LIKE I SHOULD . . .
WHAT IS THAT?
THE LETTER **H**?
YES.
H.

FOR HILO.
HELLO?
NO.
HIGH-LOW.
MY NAME IS
HILO.

COOL.
YES.
COOL.

HANG ON.
WHAT?

BURP!

I BURPED AGAIN!
YEAH. REPEAT BUSINESS!

YEAH!
REPEAT BUSINESS!
HA HA HA HA HA HA HA HA HA HA HA

HILO?
HILO!

NO, NO, NO!
HILO! WHAT'S **WRONG?!**
CAN -- CAN YOU
HEAR ME?!

STILL -- STILL BREATHING!
GOOD, YEAH , STILL --

HEART BEATING? IS THAT
YOUR HEART? **SOMETHING**
IS THUMPING IN THERE.

WHAT'S WRONG WITH YOU?!
WHAT AM I SUPPOSED TO --

ZZZZZZ
ZZZZZZ
Z z z ZZ Zz
zzZ z Z ZZ
ZZZZZZZZZ ZZ
Z Z ZZZZ ZZZ Z Z
ZZZZZZZ
ZZZZZ Z Z Z zzzzZZZ

WHUMP
ZZZZ
ZZZ
IS THIS YOUR LABORATORY?

NO. I HAD TO BRING YOU TO THE NEAREST FACILITY.
MY LAB WAS DESTROYED. THIS ONE WASN'T IN GREAT CONDITION EITHER.
WAS I HURT?
YOU WERE, HILO.
BUT I FIXED YOU UP.
THANK YOU, DR. HORIZON.

IS THE BATTLE OVER? DID I WIN?
NO.
RAZORWARK IS STILL OUT THERE. . . .
AND HE'S HEADING DIRECTLY TOWARD FARALON.
HILO!
WAIT!
I'M SORRY! I'M SO SORRY!
I SHOULD HAVE STOPPED HIM!
I'M SORRY!

DON'T BE SORRY! YOU FOUGHT AS HARD AS YOU COULD!
NOT HARD ENOUGH! I HAVE TO STOP RAZORWARK! I CAN'T LET HIM REACH FARALON!
BEEP
SHUP
BUT, DR. HORIZON ... CAN I TELL YOU A SECRET? AND PROMISE NOT TO TELL ANYONE?
OF COURSE.
I'M SCARED.

POP

AAAHH!
AAAHH!
I LOVE THAT GREETING!

YOU'RE **REALLY** AWAKE.
YEAH! DO **YOU** WANT TO FIND OUT WHERE I'M FROM?! I WANT TO FIND OUT WHERE I'M FROM! AND WHY, WHY, WHY, **WHY** I'M HERE!
C'MON! C'MON! C'MON!

NO, I GOTTA GO TO SCHOOL.
WHAT'S SCHOOL?
IT'S BORING. IT'S WHERE THEY TRY AND TEACH YOU STUFF ALL DAY.
THAT DOESN'T SOUND BORING.
ABC

YOU SHOULD STAY HERE. I'LL BE BACK AT 3.
THAT SOUNDS BORING.

CLICK

THUNK.

HEY, NERD. MOM SAYS TO COME DOWN TO BREAKFAST.
GOT IT, BROTHER DEXTER! I WILL COME TO BREAKFAST!
ABBOT

WHO WERE YOU TALKING TO BEFORE?
TALKING? NO, NO, NO, I WAS SINGING ALONG TO THE MUSIC.

YOU'RE NOT PLAYING ANY MUSIC.
UH -- **HEY!** CAN I BORROW YOUR GUITAR?

WHAT?! NO! DO NOT **TOUCH** MY GUITAR! DO NOT EVEN **THINK** OF EVER, EVER, **EVER** TOUCHING MY GUITAR!

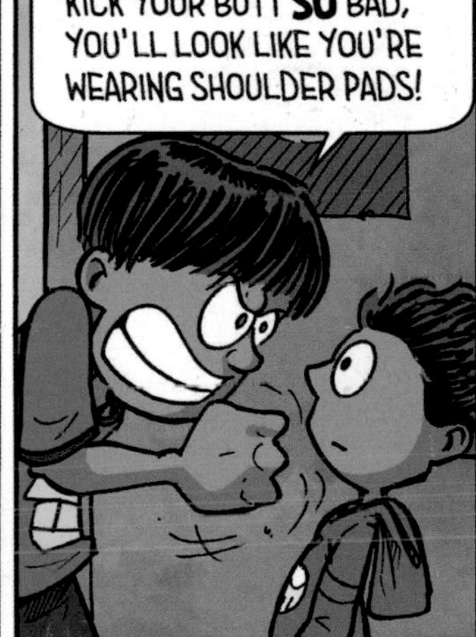
TOUCH MY GUITAR AND I WILL KICK YOUR BUTT **SO** BAD, YOU'LL LOOK LIKE YOU'RE WEARING SHOULDER PADS!

SLAM

HILO?

YOU SHOVED ME INTO A CLOSET.

YEAH. SORRY. I COULDN'T LET MY BROTHER SEE YOU.
WHY? DID HE THINK I TOUCHED HIS GUITAR?

LISTEN ... NO ONE CAN SEE YOU. AT LEAST NOT UNTIL WE FIGURE OUT SOME MORE STUFF ABOUT YOU.
BUT I WANT TO GO TO SCHOOL.

YOU CAN'T. YOU AREN'T -- WHAT DO THEY CALL IT? **ENROLLED?**

I WANT TO GO WITH YOU.

IT'LL BE OKAY. YOU'LL HAVE THE WHOLE HOUSE TO YOURSELF.

WHAT ABOUT **RAZORWARK?**

WHO?

RAZORWARK.
DO YOU KNOW WHO THAT IS?

NO.

I DON'T EITHER. SORRY. I **SHOULD** KNOW WHO HE IS. BUT MY MEMORY IS FULL OF HOLES. BUSTED BOOK.
WHEN I WAS SLEEPING, I REMEMBERED SOMETHING ABOUT HIM. NOW I DON'T KNOW WHAT IT WAS....

IS HE SOMEONE WHO CAN HELP YOU?

NO.

I THINK HE'S A MONSTER.

HOOM

THERE ARE NO MONSTERS HERE.
YOU'RE SAFE.
AND I'LL COME BACK.
I PROMISE.
OKAY?
OKAY.
CLACK

ENCYCLOPEDIA BRITANNICA C
ENCYCLOPEDIA BRITANNICA F
ENCYCLOPEDIA BRITANNICA
ENCYCLOPEDIA BRITANNICA G
ENCYCLOPEDIA BRITANNICA K
ENCYCLOPEDIA BRITANNICA T

SCHOOL

VANDERBILT ELEME

HEY, D.J.

AAAAH!
AAAAH!

HOW DID YOU GET HERE?
I WALKED.
BUT YOU BEAT MY BUS HERE.
I WALK VERY FAST.

AND I READ THE DICTIONARY AND SIXTEEN OF YOUR ENCYCLOPEDIAS.
YOU READ A DICTIONARY AND SIXTEEN ENCYCLOPEDIAS IN TWENTY MINUTES?

WELL, YEAH. I WOULD HAVE READ **ALL** OF YOUR ENCYCLOPEDIAS, EXCEPT **B, H, MN,** AND **XYZ** WERE MISSING. BUT, LISTEN -- I KNOW HOW TO GET ENROLLED IN SCHOOL.

I BROUGHT A RACCOON.
AAAH!

NO, I JUST NEED TO DISTRACT THEM IN THE OFFICE.
IT'S COOL. I GOT THIS.
OFFICE
OFFICE

OFFICE
OFFICE
OFFICE
OFFICE

OFFICE

I'M ENROLLED. LET'S GO.

SO, YOU MADE UP ALL OF YOUR SCHOOL RECORDS?

YES, IT WAS EASY.

HOW DID -- ?

HEY, D.J.

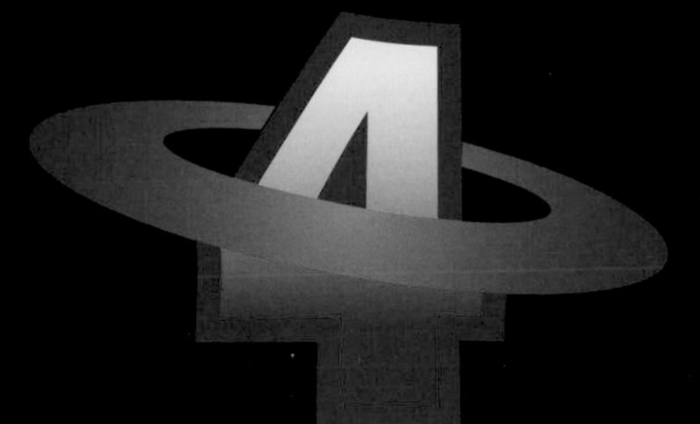

GINA

STUDENTS, SAY HELLO TO --

GINA COOPER. OUR FIRST NEW STUDENT TODAY ...

I UNDERSTAND THAT YOU WERE ORIGINALLY FROM OUR TOWN, BUT YOU MOVED AWAY A FEW YEARS AGO?
YES. WE MOVED TO NEW YORK, BUT MY DAD GOT A NEW JOB BACK HERE IN BERKE COUNTY.

MY OLD HOUSE WAS NEXT TO D. J.'S.

IS IT NICE TO BE BACK?
KIND OF. I MISS MY FRIENDS BACK IN NEW YORK.
BUT EVERYTHING HERE SEEMS THE SAME, JUST SMALLER.

THAT'S BECAUSE YOU WERE SMALLER WHEN YOU WERE LAST HERE, SO EVERYTHING APPEARED BIGGER.

UH , YES. WELL, OUR OTHER NEW STUDENT IS HILO --
AAAHH!

I LOVE THAT GREETING.

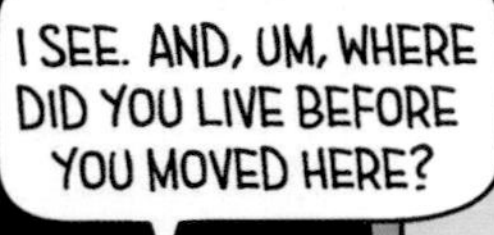
I SEE. AND, UM, WHERE DID YOU LIVE BEFORE YOU MOVED HERE?

UH-OH.

WE DON'T KNOW. WE THINK OUTER SPACE. D.J. FOUND ME AFTER I FELL FROM THE SKY.

OH NO.

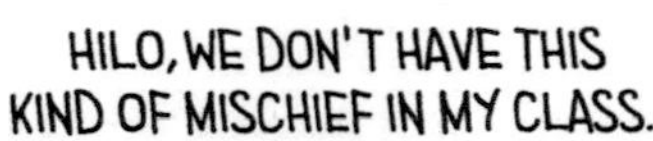
HILO, WE DON'T HAVE THIS KIND OF MISCHIEF IN MY CLASS.

OKAY.
WHAT KIND OF MISCHIEF **DO** YOU HAVE?

I SEE FROM YOUR FILE THAT YOU LIVED IN **DALLAS.**

YES! DALLAS! THE THIRD-LARGEST CITY IN TEXAS AND THE NINTH-LARGEST IN THE UNITED STATES!

DIVIDED AMONG COLLIN, DALLAS, DENTON, KAUFMAN, AND ROCKWALL COUNTIES, THE CITY HAS A POPULATION OF 1,300,350.

DUDE. YOUR PAL IS A REAL FREAK.
ANNUAL RAINFALL IS 40.9 INCHES.

SO, HILO. YOU ACTUALLY FELL FROM THE SKY?

YEAH! I WAS JUST WEARING SILVER UNDERPANTS. I **REALLY** LIKE THEM, BUT D. J. SAID I CAN'T WALK AROUND IN THEM. NOW THAT I'M OUT AND ABOUT, I CAN SEE THAT NOBODY IS WEARING SILVER UNDERPANTS.

YOU'RE FUNNY.
YEAH! HEH! HE JUST NEVER STOPS, Y'KNOW, JOKING AROUND.

WELL, I LIVE DOWN THIS WAY ON ELM. HILO, DO YOU LIVE NEAR D. J.'S HOUSE?

I LIVE **IN** D. J.'S HOUSE. BUT DON'T TELL HIS FAMILY. THEY AREN'T SUPPOSED TO KNOW.
HA! **SEE?!** ALWAYS JOKING!

BUT, UM, GINA ... MAYBE YOU COULD COME OVER LATER. OR I COULD COME OVER TO YOUR NEW HOUSE OR SOMETHING.
WE COULD HANG OUT.
LIKE WE USED TO.

OH, I'D LIKE THAT, BUT I CAN'T.

I . . . I HAVE TO GO HOME AND PRACTICE.

PRACTICE? PRACTICE FOR WHAT?

GINA'S HOUSE.

HEY, HEY! IT'S TIME TO FIGHT!

EVERYBODY YELL "BLUE AND WHITE!"

HEY, HEY! LET'S DO IT AGAIN! EVERYBODY YELL "GO! FIGHT! WIN!"

GO! FIGHT! WIN!
GINA, YOUR JUMPS HAVE TO BE WAY HIGHER.
AND POM-POMS UP.
GOT IT. JUMPS HIGHER. UP POM-POMS.
AND SMILE. IT'S CALLED CHEERLEADING. NOT CHEER-FROWNING.
GOT IT. LEADING, NOT FROWNING.
CHEERLEADER: A PERSON WHO LEADS SPECTATORS IN ORGANIZED CHEERING, ESPECIALLY AT ATHLETIC EVENTS!
YEAH.
YOU GET ONE SHOT AT MAKING THE CHEERLEADING SQUAD. ONE.
AND WE'RE DEFINITELY GOING TO HAVE TO FIX YOUR HAIR.
YOU'RE NOT TOUCHING MY HAIR.
AND IF MOM FINDS OUT YOU WORE JEANS TO SCHOOL INSTEAD OF THAT DRESS SHE PICKED OUT, SHE'S GOING TO BE WAY ANNOYED.
WAY ANNOYED.

SO ... YOU'RE TRYING OUT FOR CHEERLEADING?
RAH!
MY MOM IS MAKING ME. Y'KNOW, MY SISTERS ARE CHEERLEADERS, SO --

DAD!
HEY, GINA! I'M SORRY, I'VE GOT TO --

OH! HELLO, DANIEL. IT'S GOOD TO SEE YOU AGAIN.
HI, MR. COOPER. GOOD TO SEE YOU TOO.
THIS IS HILO.
AAAHH!!

UH-HUH. HELLO.

I CAN'T, KIDDO. IT'LL HAVE TO WAIT.

BUT THERE'S THAT METEOR SHOWER TONIGHT. NASA DIDN'T EVEN KNOW ABOUT IT UNTIL LAST NIGHT! DO YOU KNOW HOW **RARE** THAT IS?

YEAH. BACK AT MY OLD SCHOOL IN NEW YORK, OUR ASTRONOMY CLUB WOULD GO TO THE PLANETARIUM AND USE THE REAL BIG TELESCOPE.
WE DON'T HAVE A PLANETARIUM. OR AN ASTRONOMY CLUB.

OR A SCIENCE CLUB. OR A BOOK CLUB. OR MATHLETES.

I GOT OUT OF HAVING TO JOIN CHEERLEADING WITH MY SISTERS BECAUSE I WAS SO BUSY WITH MY OTHER STUFF.

MY MOM WANTS ME TO BE JUST LIKE MY SISTERS. ALL THEY DO IS TALK ABOUT BOYS AND CLOTHES.

WHAT DO YOU WANT?

I WANT TO GO HOME.

HILO?
WHERE DID HE -- ?
UP HERE.
C' MON UP!
HOW DID HE GET UP ON THE ROOF?
UH-OH.
CLICK
HILO?
UH-OH.
HEY!
CREAK
MY TELESCOPE!
HOW DID YOU DO THAT?
IT WAS EASY! ALL THE PIECES FIT. I **LIKE** IT WHEN ALL THE PIECES FIT.
TELESCOPE

EXCEPT THESE. YOU DON'T NEED THEM.

DO **NOT** EAT THOSE.
WHY?
IT USUALLY TAKES ME AND MY DAD AN HOUR TO PUT THIS TOGETHER. AND HE'S AN ENGINEER.

YEAH! WELL, UM, I GUESS THIS WILL KEEP YOU BUSY! MAYBE YOU WON'T HAVE TO BE A CHEERLEADER!

NO. MY MOM WON'T LET ME PLAY SOCCER UNLESS I CHEER.

YOU PLAY SOCCER NOW TOO?

YEAH. WELL, BACK HOME IN NEW YORK I DID. DO YOU PLAY ANY SPORTS?

NO.

I DON'T PLAY ANYTHING.

BUT D. J. THINKS BALLET SOUNDS PRETTY COOL.
WHAT?! NO! **YOU** SAID THAT! I DIDN'T--

AND D. J. FED ME RICE AND MILK **AND** GAVE ME THESE CLOTHES SO I'M NOT WALKING AROUND IN THE PREVIOUSLY MENTIONED SILVER UNDERPANTS.

YOU **REALLY** LIKE THOSE SILVER UNDERPANTS.
THEY ARE OUTSTANDING! DO YOU WANT TO SEE THEM?
HEY!

HA! AND I THOUGHT MOVING BACK HERE WOULD BE TOTALLY BORING.
BORING?
WELL, YEAH. THIS IS BERKE COUNTY. NOTHING NEW EVER HAPPENS HERE.

CHAPTER 5

NOTHING NEW EVER HAPPENS HERE

BOOM

CLACK

CLOCK

HEY, DO YOU GUYS WANT TO COME BACK OVER TONIGHT?

WE COULD ALL WATCH THE METEOR SHOWER.

SURE! THAT WOULD BE AWESOME.

YOU HEAR THAT?

HEAR WHAT?

WAIT. NOT **HEAR.**
FEEL.
I FELT IT.

SOMETHING IS WRONG.
I HAVE TO GO.
NOW.

HILO?

HILO!

MAYBE HE HAD TO GO TO THE BATHROOM. HE COULD HAVE JUST HAVE USED OURS.
I NEED TO -- I HAVE TO --

I HAVE TO GO AFTER HIM.

WHAT ARE YOU DOING? WHY -- **WHOA!**

WHAT IS THAT?

IT'S A BIG HOLE.

I SEE THAT. BUT IT LOOKS JUST LIKE --

NOT LIKE ME.

ROAAR!

AAAAHH!

AAAAA A AA A AA A
AAA A AA AAHH!!

WHAT IS THAT?!
IT'S A RANT!

A WHAT?!
A RANT!
A CYBERNETIC FORMICIDAE! A ROBOT ANT!
THEY'RE CALLED **RANTS!**

HOW DO YOU KNOW THAT?!

I DON'T REMEMBER!

BOOM
POOF
POOF

BLAM

TZAAAACK
CREE OOCK!
GROOM

HOW DID YOU DO THAT?

I DON'T KNOW.

IT'S BECAUSE YOU **REALLY** FELL FROM THE SKY.

D.J., YOU DROPPED YOUR BAG.

THANKS.
HILO ... WHERE ... WHERE **ARE** YOU FROM?

I DON'T REMEMBER.

CLACK

BLAM

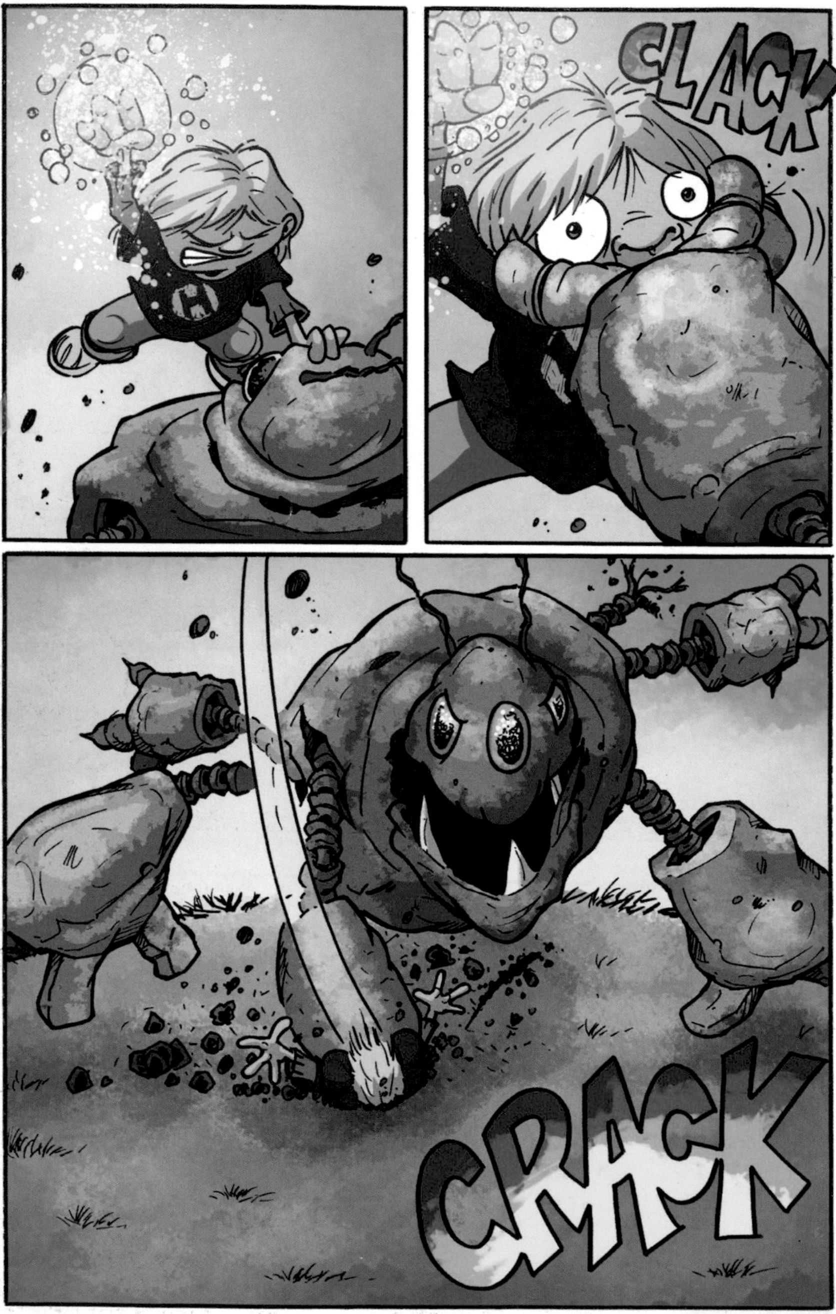

CLACK

CRACK

HILO!

BLAM

SLIP

BOOM

D.J., ARE YOU OKAY?!
I'M FINE.

WHAT ABOUT HILO?
IS HE -- IS HE OKAY?

NOT
EXACTLY.

CHAPTER

DIG

NO **MORE!!** NO MORE **DESTRUCTION!** NO MORE **DEATH!**

NO MORE **RAZORWARK!**

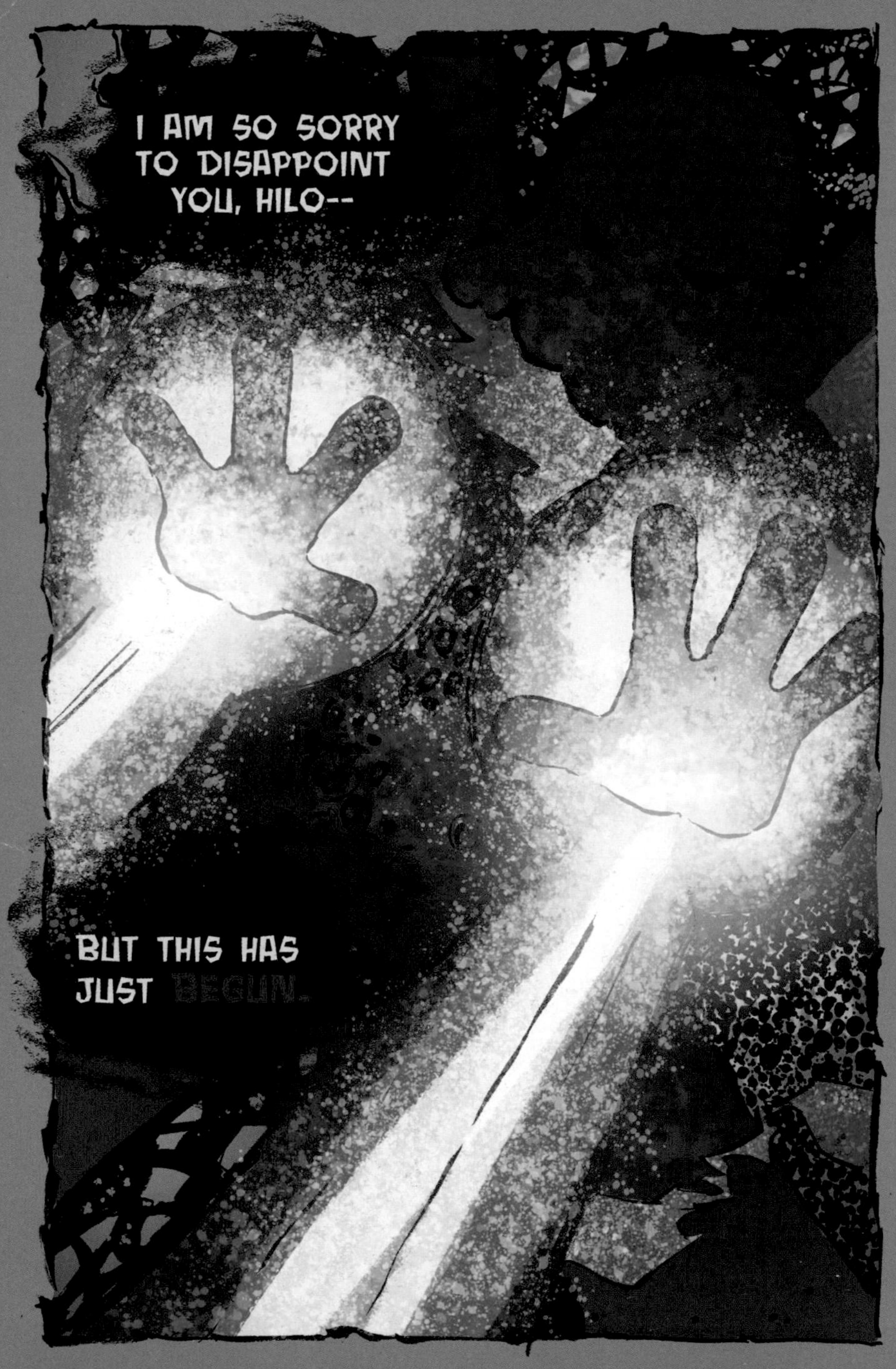
I AM SO SORRY TO DISAPPOINT YOU, HILO--
BUT THIS HAS JUST BEGUN.

HEY. HEAR THAT? HILO'S TALKING AGAIN.
YOU THINK HE'S DREAMING?
CLUB HOUSE
MAYBE.
WHAT'S THAT NAME HE KEEPS SAYING?
DR. HORIZON? I THINK HE'S A FRIEND. FIXES HIM WHEN HE'S HURT.
NO.
I MEANT THAT **OTHER** NAME HE SAID.
RAZORWARK.
YEAH. WHO IS THAT?
HILO SAID . . . HE WAS A **MONSTER.**
LOOK, LOOK, LOOK! HE'S AWAKE!
HILO?
HEY.

HEY.
HEY.
HOW ARE YOU FEELING?

I'M FEELING GOOD! WHAT HAPPENED TO THE RANT?

D.J. SHOVED HIM OFF A CLIFF.

OUTSTANDING!

YEAH, BUT LISTEN ... WE THINK WE KNOW WHAT YOU ARE.
SORT OF.

YEAH.

YEAH.
YOU'RE A **ROBOT.**

REALLY?
YOU THINK SO?

YEAH...

WE'RE PRETTY SURE.
WHOA!
LOOK AT ME!
I'M A **ROBOT!** THAT IS **OUTSTANDING!** 
OKAY. YEAH. MAYBE. BUT YOU'RE A REALLY, **REALLY** BROKEN ROBOT.

TRUE, TRUE, BUT IT DOESN'T TAKE AWAY FROM HOW UNBELIEVABLY COOL IT IS THAT I'M AN ACTUAL **ROBOT.**

AND I DON'T THINK I'M BROKEN.

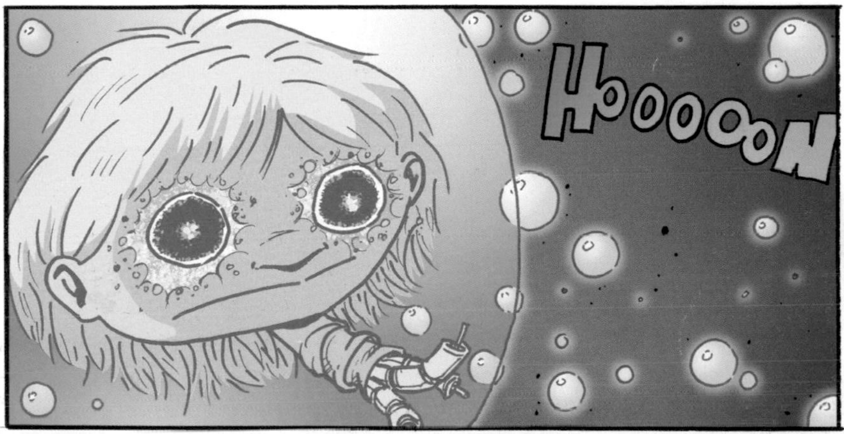
HOOOOON

CLACK

RATTLE-ATTLE
ATTLE-ATTLE

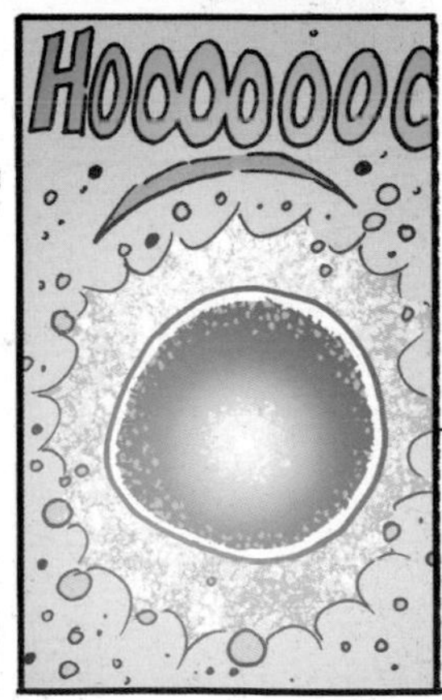
HOOOOOOO

BWOOP

BWOOOOP

BWOOP

PLEP
PLEP
PLEP
PL
PLEP
PLEP

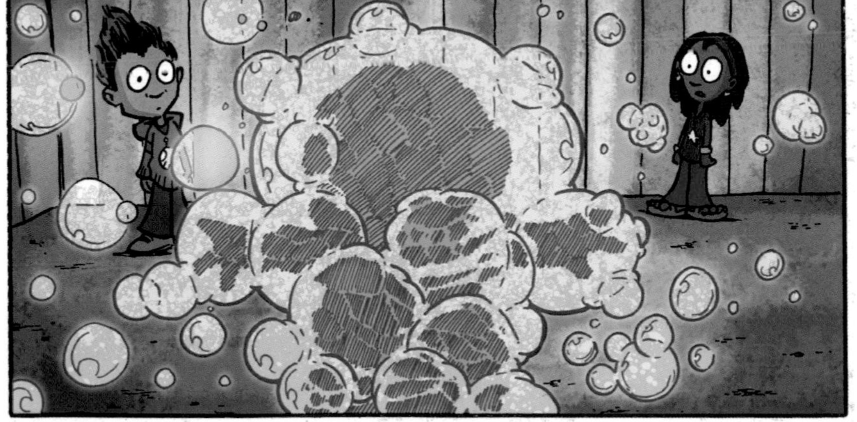

WOW.

I KNOW!
ALL THE PIECES FIT!

SO YOU'RE A ROBOT. MAYBE YOU'RE NOT FROM SPACE. MAYBE YOU **ARE** A GOVERNMENT EXPERIMENT. MAYBE YOU ESCAPED AND THEY SENT THE RANT AFTER YOU.

I DON'T THINK THE GOVERNMENT COULD MAKE HIM, D. J. HE'S TOO ADVANCED. THEY STILL HAVEN'T MADE A FLYING CAR. YOU THINK THEY CAN MAKE A BOY WHO CAN SHOOT LASERS FROM HIS HANDS?
HOLY MACKEREL -- I FORGOT ABOUT THE LASERS! HOW OUTSTANDING ARE MY HAND LASERS?!

YEAH. HE'S GOT TO BE FROM SOMEPLACE ELSE.

I FELL THROUGH A HOLE.

WHAT?

I HAD A DREAM, BUT IT WASN'T A DREAM. IT WAS A MEMORY.
I WAS FIGHTING . . . SOMEONE.

RAZORWARK?

YES.

I WAS FIGHTING HIM. WE WERE ON OUR WORLD . . . THEN I FELL THROUGH A HOLE.

AND I LANDED HERE.

MAYBE HE'S FROM ANOTHER DIMENSION. LIKE IN THE NARNIA BOOKS. OR AN ALTERNATE REALITY LIKE IN COMICS.
YOU STILL READ COMICS?

YEAH.

COOL.

HILO, DO YOU REMEMBER **WHY** YOU WERE FIGHTING RAZORWARK?

HE WAS TRYING TO HURT THEM.
HURT WHO?
MY FRIENDS.
I DON'T LET ANYONE DO THAT.

WE HAVE TO GO.

C'MON!
WHERE NOW?
CLUB HOUSE
BACK TO WHERE WE FOUND THE RANT! IT ATTACKED US BECAUSE WE INTERRUPTED IT!

THIS IS NOT JUST A CRATER!
IT'S A **HOLE!**
THAT RANT WAS **DIGGING!**
WHY?!
YEAH, WHAT WAS IT LOOKING FOR?!
I DON'T KNOW!
CHUG CHUG
CHUG CHUG
BONG
IS THAT METAL?
WHAT DID YOU FIND?!
I DON'T KNOW!
YOU NEED HELP?!

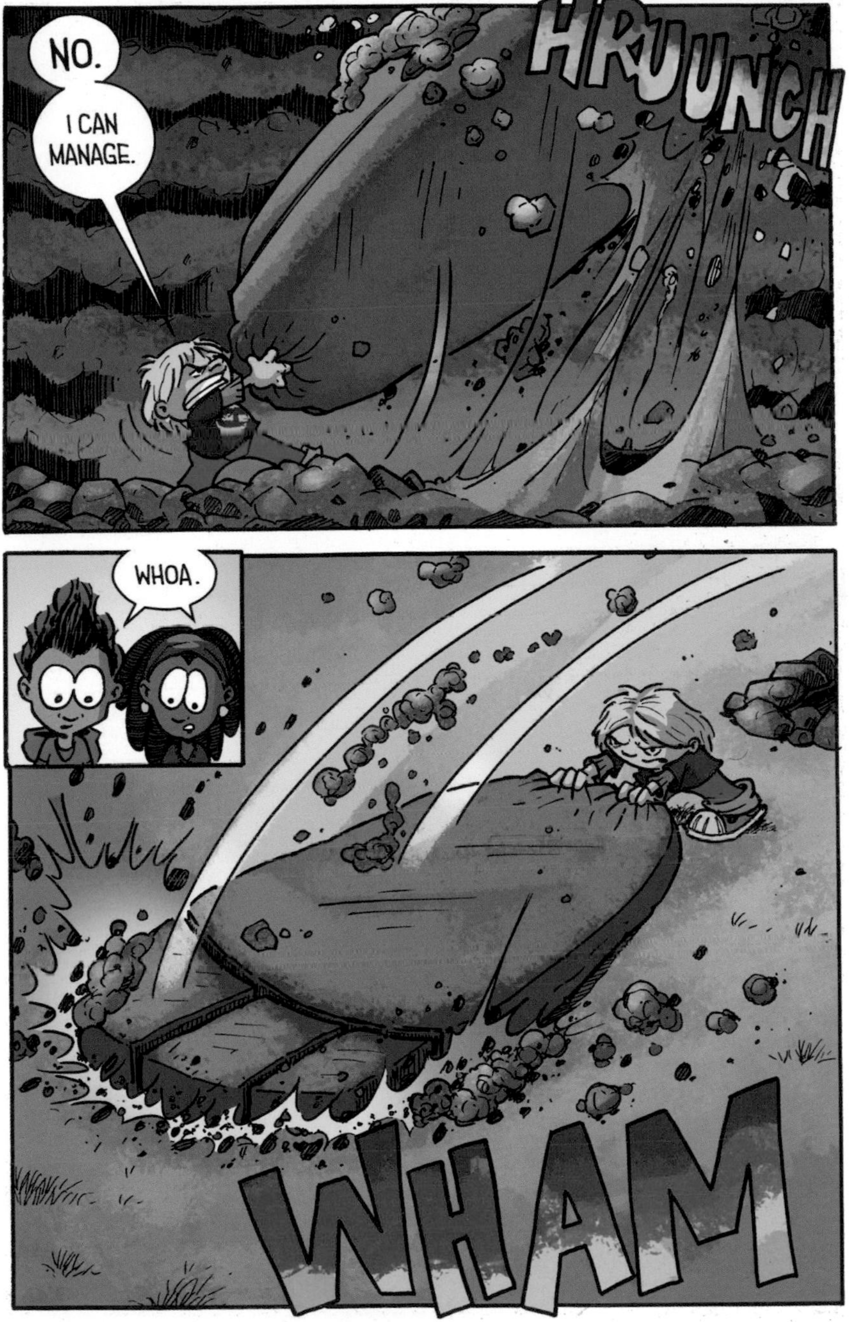

WHOA.

WHAM

IT'S --

IT'S A **FOOT!**

A **BIG** FOOT.

OUTSTANDING!

COULD BE AN OCTOPED! THEN WE'VE GOT **SEVEN** MORE FEET TO FIND.

OCTOPED! I **SO** WANTED TO USE THAT WORD IN A SENTENCE TODAY, AND **BOOM!**
OCTOPED!
OKAY, OKAY, BUT NOW WHAT? WE CAN'T JUST LEAVE IT HERE.

NO. WE HAVE TO PUT IT IN YOUR ROOM.

NO.

YOUR ROOM?

NO.

WELL, IT'S GOTTA GO IN SOMEBODY'S ROOM.
WAIT, I KNOW! I GOT A ROOM! THE CLUBHOUSE!

THIS IS **GREAT!** AND NOT JUST BECAUSE IT PERFECTLY FITS A GIANT METAL FOOT AND SMELLS LIKE SQUIRREL POOP. IT'S 'CAUSE IT'S OVERRUN WITH A **TON** OF SPIDERS.

OCTOPEDS.

OKAY, WE'VE GOT THE FOOT HIDDEN. WE'VE GOT PLENTY OF SPIDERS, PLENTY OF SQUIRREL-POOP SMELL -- WHICH I'M BEGINNING TO THINK **ISN'T** A GOOD THING AFTER ALL.

BUT NOW ALL WE HAVE TO DO IS WAIT.
AND LISTEN.
THWACK
LISTEN?

SORRY. NOT LISTEN. **FEEL.**
AND NOT **WE.**
JUST ME.
I FEEL.

FEEL FOR WHAT?

OTHERS.
OTHERS LIKE THE RANT. THEY'LL WANT THE FOOT. OR **OTHER** FEET. I'LL FEEL 'EM WHEN THEY SHOW UP.

I DON'T KNOW HOW I KNOW. I JUST KNOW. BUSTED BOOK MEMORY.

C'MON!
YOU FEEL A RANT COMING?!

NO! IT'S ALMOST DINNERTIME! LET'S GO TO D. J.'S HOUSE!

I THOUGHT YOU WERE WAITING FOR YOUR "FEELINGS"?!

I CAN DO THAT ANYWHERE! BUT DINNER AT YOUR HOUSE CAN ONLY BE AT YOUR HOUSE!

DO WE HAVE TO?! I'D MUCH RATHER BE ATTACKED BY A GIANT ROBOT INSECT!

I REALLY WOULD.

IS THERE JUICE?
IN THE GARAGE REFRIGERATOR.
WHERE ARE MY **WHITE** TIGHTS?
IN THE DRYER.
IS THIS STILL GOOD?
WHAT IS IT?
I DON'T KNOW.
SMELL IT.

DOES YOUR FAMILY EVER SIT DOWN?
NO.
AWESOME.

DAD, CAN I GET A LIFT TO STUDY GROUP?
YES.

BUT I THOUGHT LOUIS WAS TAKING YOU.
I'VE GOT TENNIS PRACTICE, AND I'M TAKING JENNIFER TO DANCE CLASS.
THE CHICKEN IS REALLY GOOD, MOM.
YEAH!

IT'S OUTSTANDING!
WHO IS THIS?

PHILO.
HILO.

AAAHH!

HE'S A FRIEND OF D.J.'S.
D.J.?
YES.

WHAT FRIENDS?
D.J. HASN'T HAD A FRIEND OVER SINCE GINA MOVED AWAY.

HEY.
HOLY MACKEREL -- GINA'S HERE! MOM! GINA'S HERE.

YES, DEXTER. SHE MOVED BACK LAST WEEK.
WHO?
GINA.

WHERE DID YOU MOVE FROM?
I FELL FROM THE SKY.

TEXAS. HE'S FROM TEXAS!
IT'S THE CORE OF THE LARGEST INLAND METROPOLITAN AREA IN THE UNITED STATES THAT LACKS ANY NAVIGABLE LINK TO THE SEA.

YOU DON'T HAVE AN ACCENT.
SHOULD I?

MOST PEOPLE FROM TEXAS HAVE AN ACCENT. WERE YOU BORN THERE?
I DON'T THINK SO. I FELL FROM THE SKY.
HA HA HA HA! HILO'S ALWAYS MAKING JOKES.
HE WASN'T JOKING. HE SAID HE FELL FROM THE SKY. TWICE.

THIS IS BAD. LISA IS THE SMARTEST ONE HERE. AND THE ONLY ONE WHO REALLY PAYS ATTENTION. HILO'S GOTTA ACT NORMAL.

HILO IS EATING HIS NAPKIN.

SPIT IT OUT.
FWAAAH!
HEY -- HEY --
WHAT IS **THAT?!**
APRIL
LOUIS
DEXTER
JENNIFER
LISA

THE FAMILY CALENDAR. THAT WAY WE CAN KEEP EVERYONE'S ACTIVITIES STRAIGHT.
JUICE

D. J.'S NOT ON THE CALENDAR.

D. J. DOESN'T DO ANYTHING .

HILO IS DRINKING SALAD DRESSING.

GLUK

SPIT

YOU'RE WEIRD.
ARE YOU WEARING D.J.'S OLD CLOTHES?
NOPE! HE'S NOT!
HE **IS.** I KNOW 'CAUSE THEY USED TO BE **MY** OLD CLOTHES.

WHO'S WEARING D.J.'S CLOTHES?
THEY'RE DEXTER'S CLOTHES.
PHILO IS.

I DON'T THINK HE'S FROM TEXAS.

DID HE DRINK AN ENTIRE GALLON OF MILK?
AND THOSE ARE **MY** OLD SNEAKERS.

LOUIS HAS A GIRLFRIEND!

EXCUSE ME?
I DO NOT.
IT'S BECKY DAHLMAN.
TOTALLY BECKY DAHLMAN.
WHO'S BECKY DAHLMAN?
LOUIS'S GIRLFRIEND.
IT'S **NOT** BECKY DAHLMAN!
BUT YOU **DO** HAVE A GIRLFRIEND...
GO, GO, GO.
THANK YOU FOR DINNER!
THAT WAS GREAT! WE SHOULD HAVE DINNER AGAIN RIGHT NOW! YOUR FAMILY IS OUTSTANDING!
I'M GLAD SOMEONE THINKS SO.
YOU DON'T LIKE YOUR FAMILY?

OF COURSE I DO. I JUST DON'T LIKE LIVING WITH THEM SOMETIMES.

WHY DON'T YOU LEAVE?

WHAT? WHAT DO YOU MEAN?

IF YOU DON'T LIKE IT HERE, YOU COULD GO. MOVE.
VACATE : VERB. TO CEASE TO OCCUPY OR HOLD; GIVE UP.
ABBOT

HILO . . . I'M NOT GOING TO RUN AWAY.
WHY?

LOTS OF REASONS. BUT MOSTLY . . . BECAUSE IT WOULDN'T FIX ANYTHING .

DO YOU UNDERSTAND?
YOU LOOK CONFUSED.

NO...IT'S NOT THAT.
IT'S...

BURP!

HA HA HA HA!
REPEAT BUSINESS!
WHY DO BOYS ALWAYS LAUGH AT BURPING?

HILO!
HANG ON! HANG ON! IT'S OKAY! IT HAPPENED BEFORE!

YES. STILL BREATHING. STILL PUMPING.

HE'S ASLEEP.
ZZZZ ZZZZ ZZZZZ

WOW. IT'S A GOOD THING HE DIDN'T PASS OUT IN FRONT OF YOUR FAMILY. THAT WOULD HAVE BEEN HARD TO EXPLAIN.
YEAH.

BUT THEY PROBABLY WOULD HAVE BEEN TOO BUSY TO NOTICE.
HA!
YEAH, THEY DO HAVE A LOT GOING ON.

BUT THEY AREN'T **SO** BAD ... ARE THEY?

NO.

THEY'RE A LOT LIKE YOU, ACTUALLY.
WHAT?

THEY'RE ALL GOOD AT A BUNCH OF STUFF.
LIKE YOU.
BUT NOT ME.
I'M PRETTY BORING.

YOU'RE NOT BORING.
I AM.

I KNOW THE ONLY REASON YOU'RE HANGING OUT WITH ME IS BECAUSE OF HILO.
HE SURE ISN'T BORING.

D.J., THAT'S NOT TRUE. I --

WE USED TO BE FRIENDS. THEN YOU MOVED AWAY. AND ...
YOU CHANGED.
BUT THAT'S OKAY. YOU'RE SUPPOSED TO CHANGE.

BUT I DIDN'T.
I'M JUST LIKE THE CLUBHOUSE.
AND BERKE COUNTY.
I'M THE SAME.
I'M **ALWAYS** GOING TO BE THE SAME.

D.J....

YOU SHOULD GO.
YOUR PARENTS ARE GOING TO WONDER WHERE YOU ARE.
AND YOU'RE GOING TO MISS THE METEOR SHOWER.

I NEED TO STAY WITH HILO.

I'LL SEE YOU TOMORROW.

CLICK

CHAPTER 7

RUN

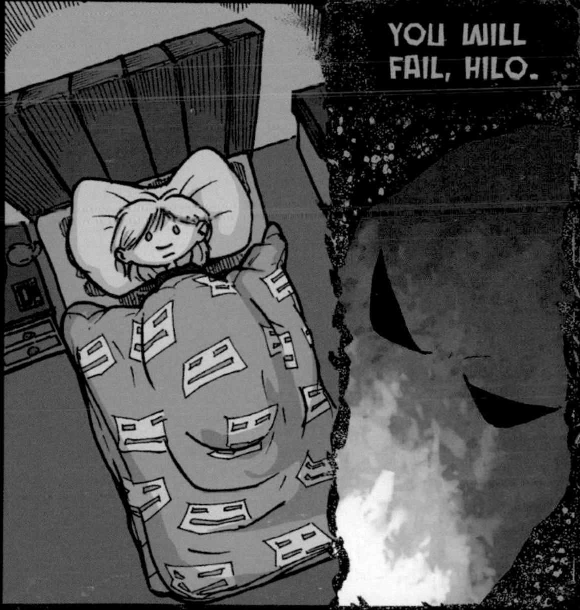

YOU CAN'T STOP US ALL.
I DON'T NEED TO! I JUST HAVE TO STOP **YOU!**
YOU WON'T. YOU ARE TOO SMALL. TOO SCARED.
AND AS YOU CAN SEE . . .
YOU ARE TOO LATE.
NO.

NO.

AAH!
AAH.

WE HAVE TO GO.

WHAT IS IT?

THOSE WEREN'T METEORS IN THAT METEOR SHOWER.

IF THEY WEREN'T METEORS, THEN WHAT WERE THEY?
SOMETHING ELSE.

HILO ATE SIX BAGELS ON THE WAY OVER, SO HE MIGHT BURP AGAIN.
THANKS FOR THE WARNING.

WHERE DID HE GO?
UH-OH.

HILO?!

SOMETHING ELSE IS COMING!

COULD YOU PLEASE TELL US NEXT TIME YOU'RE GOING TO RUN AWAY?!
OKAY!

D.J.!
WHAT?!
I MEANT IT WHEN I SAID YOU'RE NOT BORING!
WHAT?!
CONSTRUCTION
YOU'RE NOT BORING! I NEVER **EVER** THOUGHT YOU WERE BORING!
I JUST --
PLAYING SOCCER OR TENNIS OR BEING IN THE SCIENCE CLUB OR BALLET DOESN'T MAKE YOU INTERESTING!
OKAY, BUT --
AND BORING PEOPLE DON'T CHASE ROBOT BOYS WHO SHOOT **LASERS** FROM THEIR HANDS!
AND I DIDN'T THINK YOU WERE BORING **BEFORE** THE ROBOT BOY WHO SHOOTS LASERS FROM HIS HANDS SHOWED UP!
YOU'RE NOT BORING!
DO NOT ENTER!
CONSTRUCTI

OKAY?!

OKAY.

BUT YOU ARE REALLY SLOW!
I AM NOT.

BE QUIET AND RUN!

OUR FRIEND NEEDS US.

BOOM
BOOM
BOOM
BOOM

WHAT ARE THEY?
THAT'S AN ELBOW JOINT. I THINK I SEE AN OCULAR LENS AND A FINGER. IT'S LIKE THE FOOT WE FOUND.
PIECES.

MAYBE ... SOMETHING IS COMING TO EARTH LIKE YOU DID ... BUT IN PIECES.

UH-OH.
WHAT?

I THINK WE'VE GOT COMPANY.
HOLY MACKEREL.

SPROING
BUGS.
BIG ROBOT BUGS.
LIKE THE RANT.

EXCEPT THIS ONE. WHY DON'T THEY WANT IT?
OH BOY.
RUMBLE RUMBLE

RUN!
GO!
CRACK
CRAC
CRACK
CRACK CRACK
RUMBLE
RUMBLE

CLANK
BOOM

GO! I GOT THIS!
UH-OH.
CWOOSH

NO.

D.J., C'MON -- WE'VE GOT TO GET HELP! **NOW!**
HE'S ALONE DOWN THERE!
I KNOW! BUT WHAT CAN **WE** DO AGAINST THAT THING?! WE --

BUT **I** FOUND HIM! HE DOESN'T HAVE ANYONE BUT US! JUST **US** IN THE WHOLE WORLD!

D.J.!

CONSTRUCTION

POOF
FOOP
HILO?!
ARE YOU INSANE?!
ARE YOU **TOTALLY** WHACK-A-DOODLE BRAIN-DEAD CRAZY?!

GINA! WHAT ARE YOU DOING?
WHAT AM I DOING?! I'M CLIMBING A ROPE. I'M NOT JUMPING INTO A FORTY-FOOT-DEEP HOLE!

WERE YOU TRYING TO GET YOURSELF KILLED?!

SOMEONE WAS HURTING MY FRIEND.
I DON'T LET ANYONE DO THAT.
BOYS.

I --

WHERE'S HILO?
WE --

ISN'T THAT THE ELBOW JOINT?
YEAH, I --

ROOAR

BUUURP

REPEAT BUSINESS.

CLANG

GOOD NEWS.
IT SEEMS THAT I CAN FLY.
OUTSTANDING!
I KNOW, RIGHT?

HIDE.

TAK TAK
TAK TAK TAK
CLACK

TAK TAK TAK TAK
TAK TAK TAK
TAK

OCTOPED.

CLANG

TAK TAK TAK
TAK TAK TAK

HOLY MACKEREL.
ALL THE PIECES FIT.

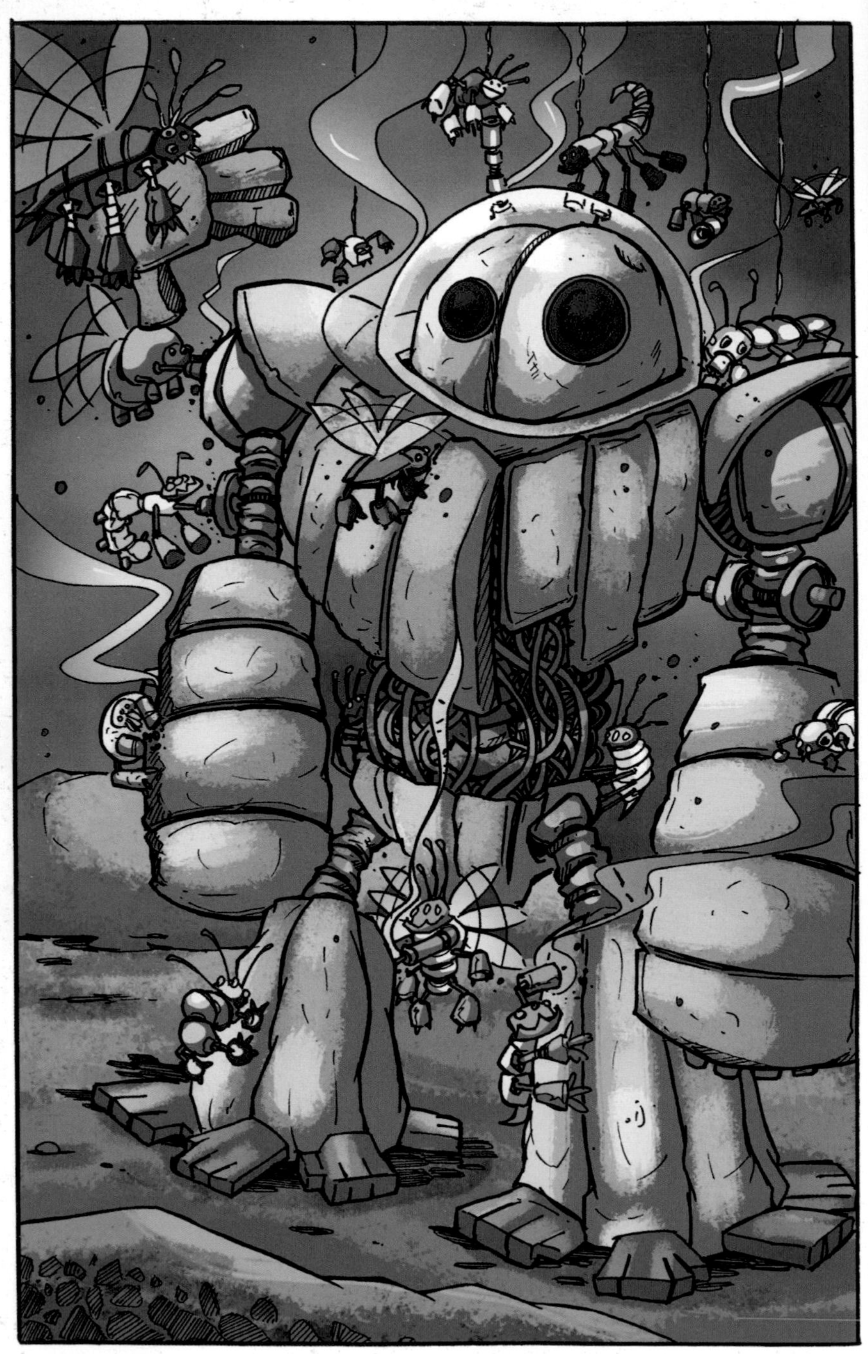

CHAPTER

I STOP THEM WHEN THEY GO WRONG

IT'S CALLED
AN OBLITERATRON.

IS THAT
BAD?

YES. OBLITERATRONS ONLY DO **ONE** THING. THEY DESTROY WORLDS.

AND ...
I REMEMBER.

THEY SERVE **RAZORWARK.**

OBLITERATRONS ARE TOO BIG TO TRAVEL. HE TELEPORTS THEM IN PIECES. THEN HE SENDS THE BUGS TO PUT THEM TOGETHER.

THIS IS MY FAULT.
RAZORWARK SENT THEM THROUGH THE HOLE I CAME OUT OF.

I REMEMBER.

JUST A LITTLE BIT . . .
IN PIECES . . .
BUT I REMEMBER.

GINA'S RIGHT.

I COME FROM ANOTHER DIMENSION.
A WORLD THAT RUNS PARALLEL TO EARTH.

WE'RE MORE TECHNOLOGICALLY ADVANCED.
ROBOTS ARE EVERYWHERE.
PEOPLE BARELY HAVE TO DO ANYTHING ANYMORE....
WE ROBOTS ... WE DO EVERYTHING TO SERVE HUMANITY.
BUT SOMETIMES ... SOME OF US ...
GO WRONG.

THAT'S WHAT I DO.

I STOP THEM WHEN THEY GO WRONG.

THE MONSTER I DREAMT I WAS FIGHTING ...
RAZORWARK.
HE'S THE MOST POWERFUL ROBOT ON OUR WORLD.

HE DOESN'T BELIEVE MACHINES SHOULD SERVE **ANYONE** ANYMORE.
HE'S LEADING A WAR AGAINST ALL LIVING THINGS.

HE LAUNCHED HIS BIGGEST ... HIS MOST DEVASTATING ATTACK ON **FARALON.**

WHAT'S FARALON?

THE CAPITAL CITY OF MY WORLD.
MY HOME.
I TRIED TO STOP HIM.
YOU WON'T. YOU ARE TOO SMALL. TOO SCARED.
BUT I FAILED.
AND YOU ARE TOO LATE.

IT'S GONE.
HE DESTROYED FARALON.
I FAILED THEM ALL.

THEN WE FOUGHT. **HARD.**
WE RIPPED A HOLE FROM OUR WORLD INTO THIS ONE.
AND YOU FELL THROUGH IT.
NO.
I **JUMPED** THROUGH IT.
I RAN AWAY.
RAZORWARK SCARES ME.
SO...I RAN AWAY.
I SHOULDN'T HAVE DONE THAT.

YOU WERE SCARED.
THAT'S OKAY.

BUT RUNNING AWAY DIDN'T FIX ANYTHING, DID IT?

AND NOW HE'S SENT THE OBLITERATRON TO DESTROY YOUR WORLD.
I CAN'T BE SCARED. I CAN'T RUN AWAY.

AND I DON'T LET **ANYONE** HURT MY FRIENDS.

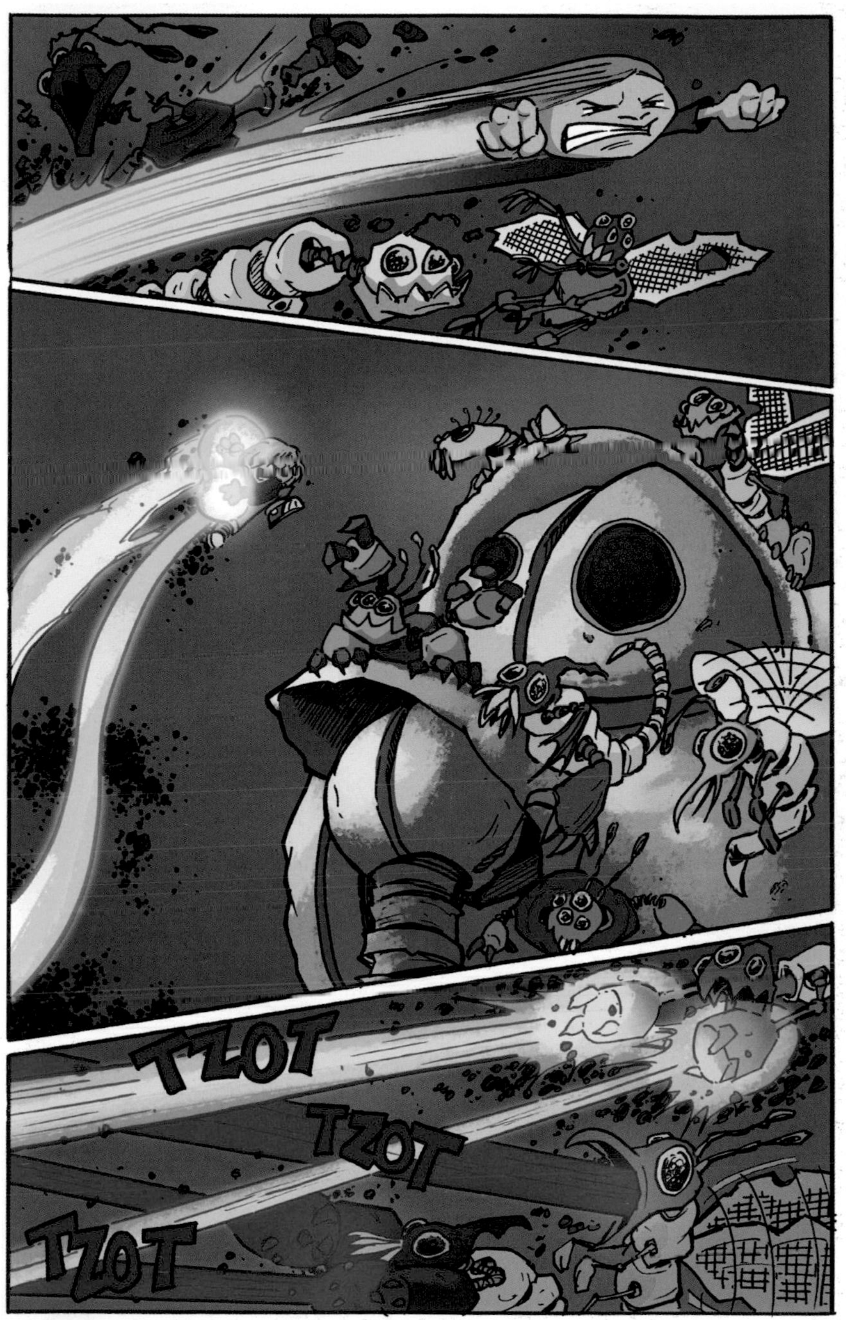
TZOT
TZOT
TZOT

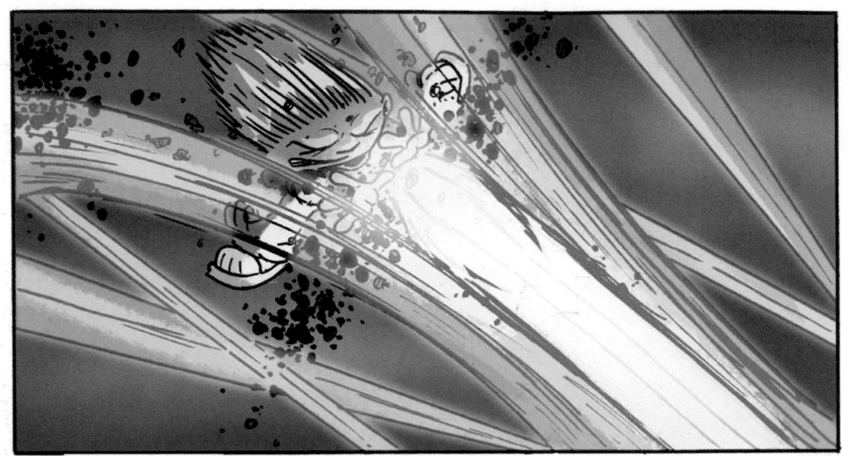

C'MON. WE GOTTA GET DOWN THERE!
AND DO **WHAT?**

BEAT ON SOME BUGS!
A **THOUSAND** OF THEM?!

HILO NEEDS US!
OKAY! BUT WE'RE NOT JUST GOING TO DIVE INTO A HALF TON OF ANGRY ROBOTIC INSECTS! WE NEED A PLAN!

RUN.
THAT'S YOUR PLAN?

C'MON!

C'MON!

C'MON!

THIS THING LOOKS LIKE IT'S ALMOST READY TO START --

HOOOOOM

YOU SEE THAT?! IT'S AWAKE!
YEAH!
BUT WE CAN'T DO MUCH ABOUT IT **RIGHT NOW!**

ROOAR

CRANG

CLANG

WHUMP

GRRRRRR

CLANG

GET!

OFF!
CLANG

OF!
CLANG

HER!
CHUNG

YOU!

COCKROACH!
CLUNG

CLACK

WHOOSH

UH-OH.

ROAARR

D.J.! HIS **MOUTH!**
LIKE HILO DID!
GO FOR ITS --

CHUNK

FLOP

URK

BUUUUUUUURP

CHUNG

REPEAT BUSINESS.
OH YEAH.

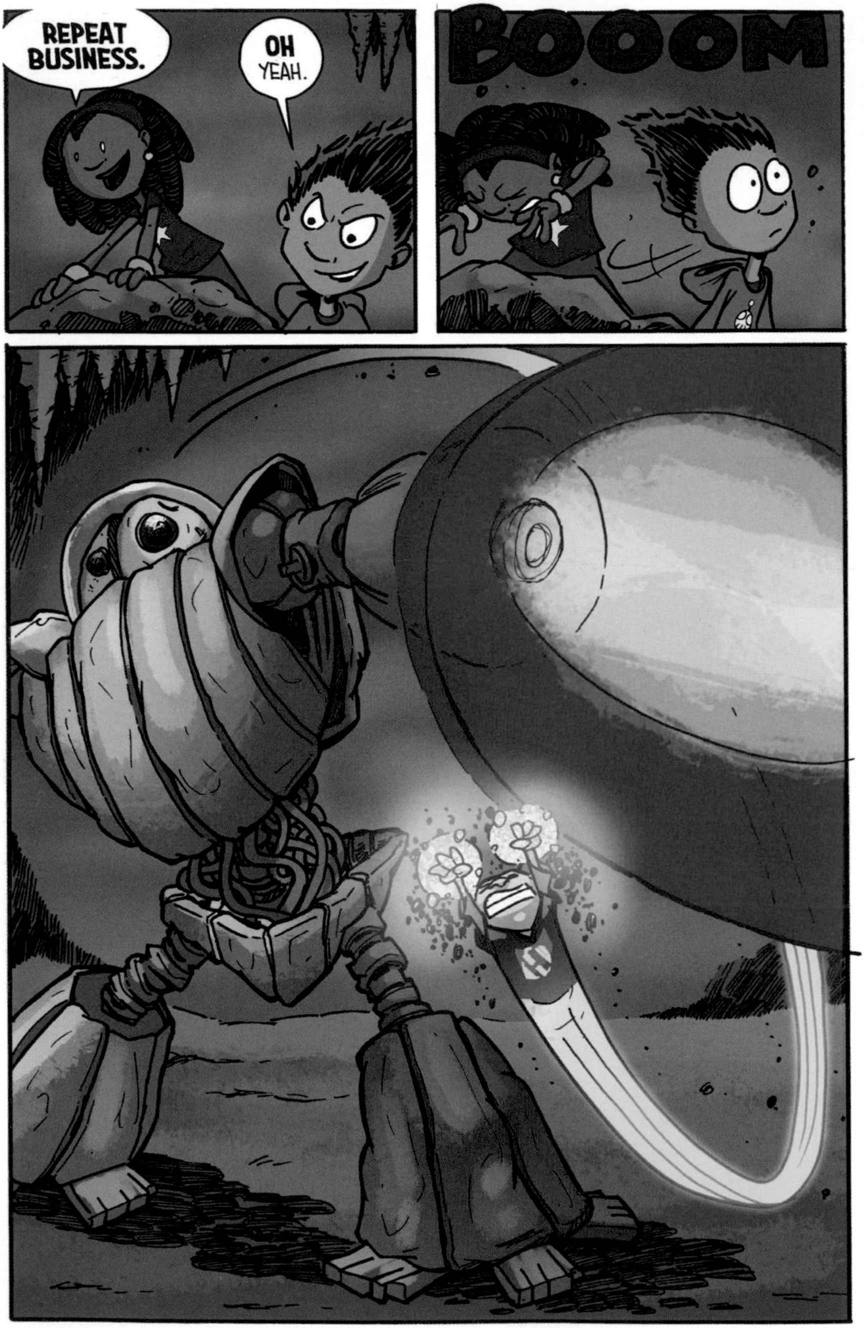

BOOOM

BOOM

RUMBLE RUMBLE

STOP!
DON'T DO THIS! YOU DON'T HAVE TO DESTROY THE EARTH!
I OBEY MY ORDERS. I AM HERE TO BRING YOU HOME.
WHAT?! THEN I'LL GO! TAKE ME! I WON'T FIGHT! JUST LEAVE THIS WORLD ALONE!
IT IS NOT THAT SIMPLE, HILO.
RAZORWARK KNOWS YOU WELL. YOU WILL FLEE BACK HERE.
I AM TO DESTROY THIS PLACE. AND YOU WILL HAVE NOWHERE TO RUN.

HE … HE WANTS YOU TO DESTROY THIS ENTIRE WORLD … JUST TO GET TO **ME?**

TO GET TO YOU …

RAZORWARK WOULD LAY WASTE TO **HUNDREDS** OF PLANETS.

YOU SHOULD NEVER HAVE RUN, HILO.

TZAACK

STOP. THIS IS NEEDLESS.
I WILL DESTROY THIS WORLD.
BOOM
AND THEN WE WILL GO HOME.

CRACK

HILO!

OW.
HANG ON!
I'VE GOT YOU!

I . . . CAN'T HURT HIM.
IF I CAN'T HURT HIM,
I CAN'T STOP HIM.

THEY'RE WEAK ON THE **INSIDE.**
WHAT?

THE ROBOTS! IF YOU CAN GET **INSIDE,** THEN YOU CAN --
MAKE SOME REPEAT BUSINESS.

OUTSTANDING! WHAT DO YOU NEED US TO DO?
HANG ON!
HEY!

WHAT ARE YOU DOING?!
GETTING YOU OUT OF THERE.

AND DOING MY JOB.

I STOP **BAD MACHINES.**

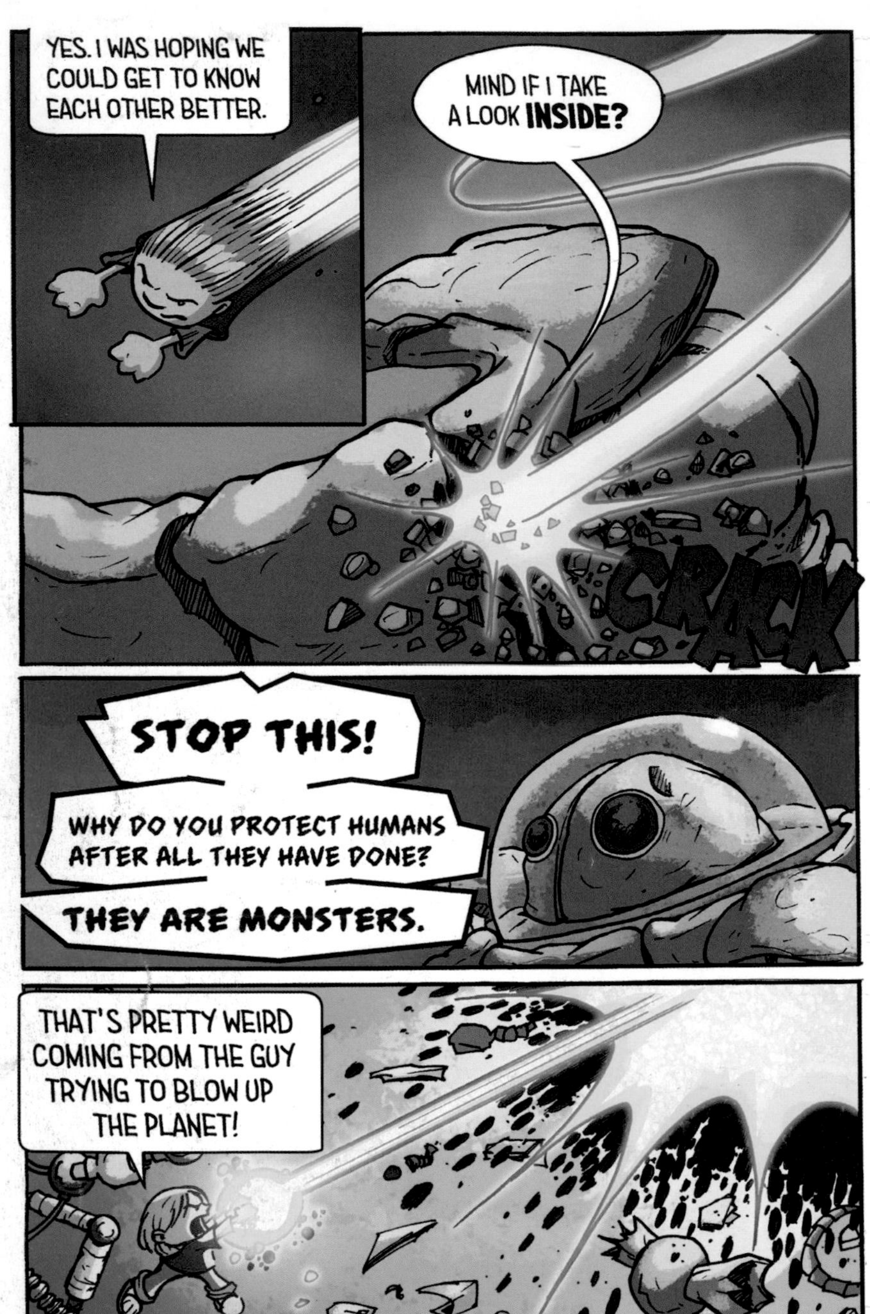
YES. I WAS HOPING WE COULD GET TO KNOW EACH OTHER BETTER.
MIND IF I TAKE A LOOK **INSIDE?**
CRACK
STOP THIS!
WHY DO YOU PROTECT HUMANS AFTER ALL THEY HAVE DONE?
THEY ARE MONSTERS.
THAT'S PRETTY WEIRD COMING FROM THE GUY TRYING TO BLOW UP THE PLANET!

ENOUGH.
ENOUGH!
ENOUGH!

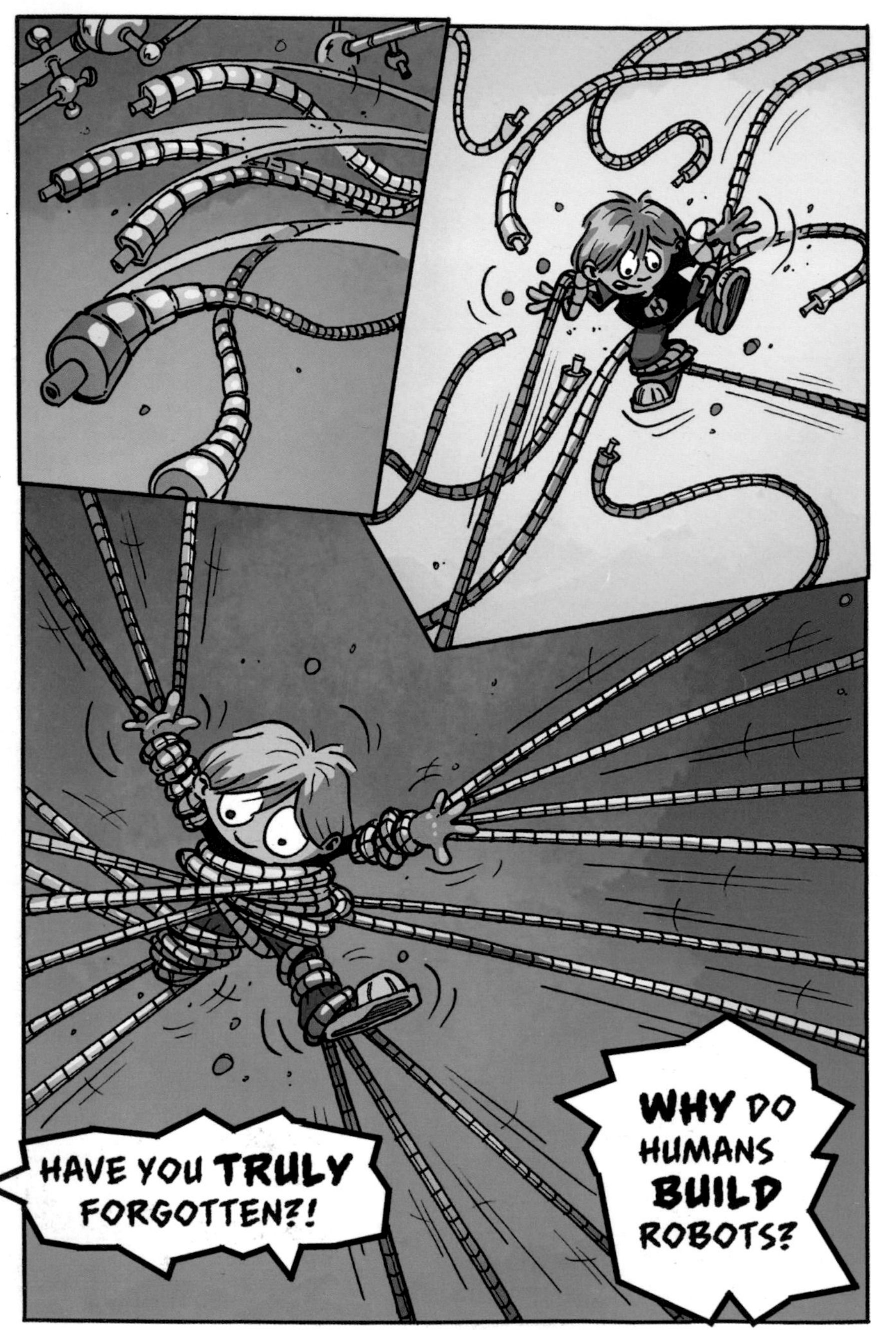
HAVE YOU TRULY FORGOTTEN?!
WHY DO HUMANS BUILD ROBOTS?

THEY NEED OUR HELP!

YES. SIMPLE HELP AT FIRST.

THEN ...ALL THEY DO IS USE US TO DESTROY.

THEY MADE YOU DESTROY.

WE ARE THE SAME, HILO.
YOU. ME.
RAZORWARK.
WE ARE THE SAME.

NO.

NO!

I DON'T KNOW EXACTLY WHAT I AM --

BUT I **DO** KNOW --
WE ARE NOT THE SAME!

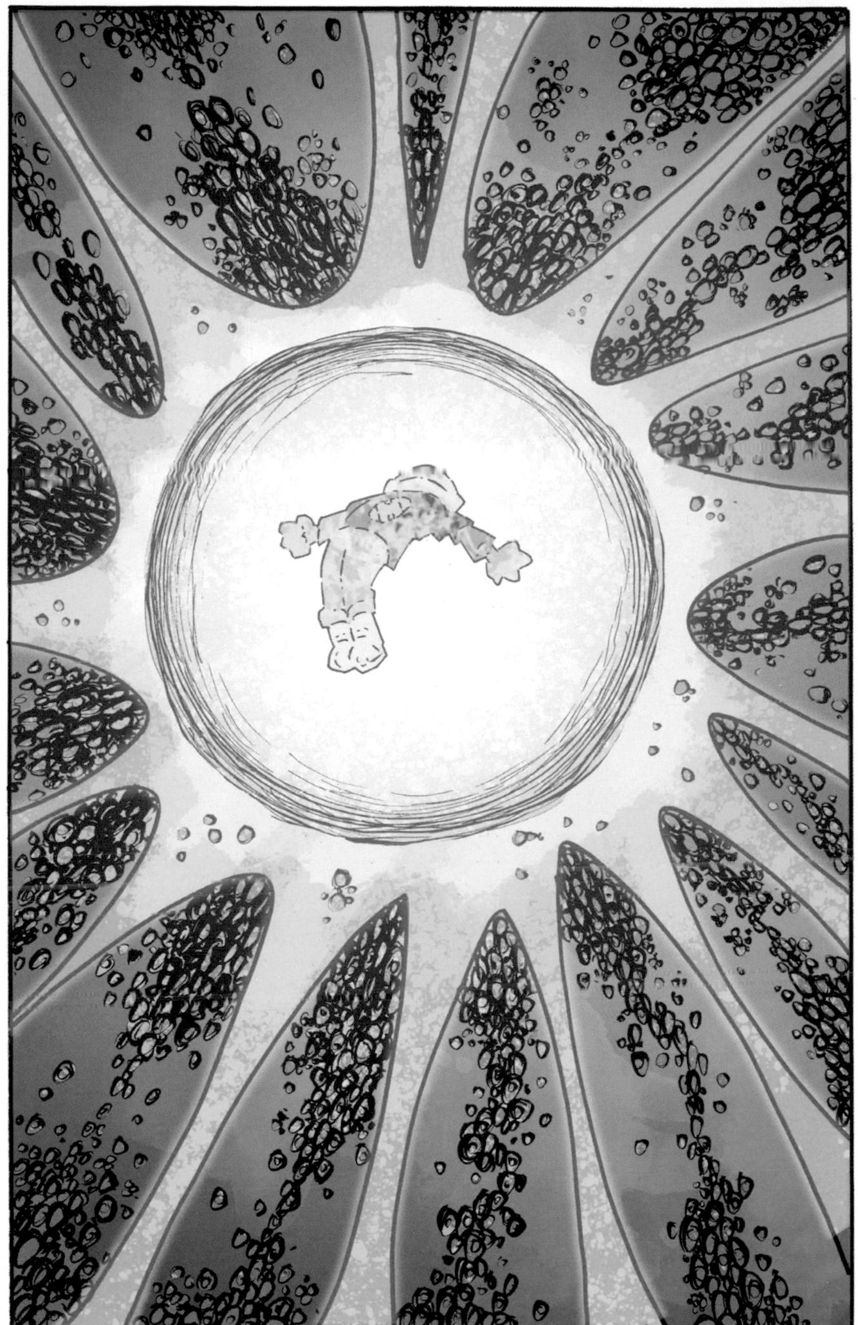

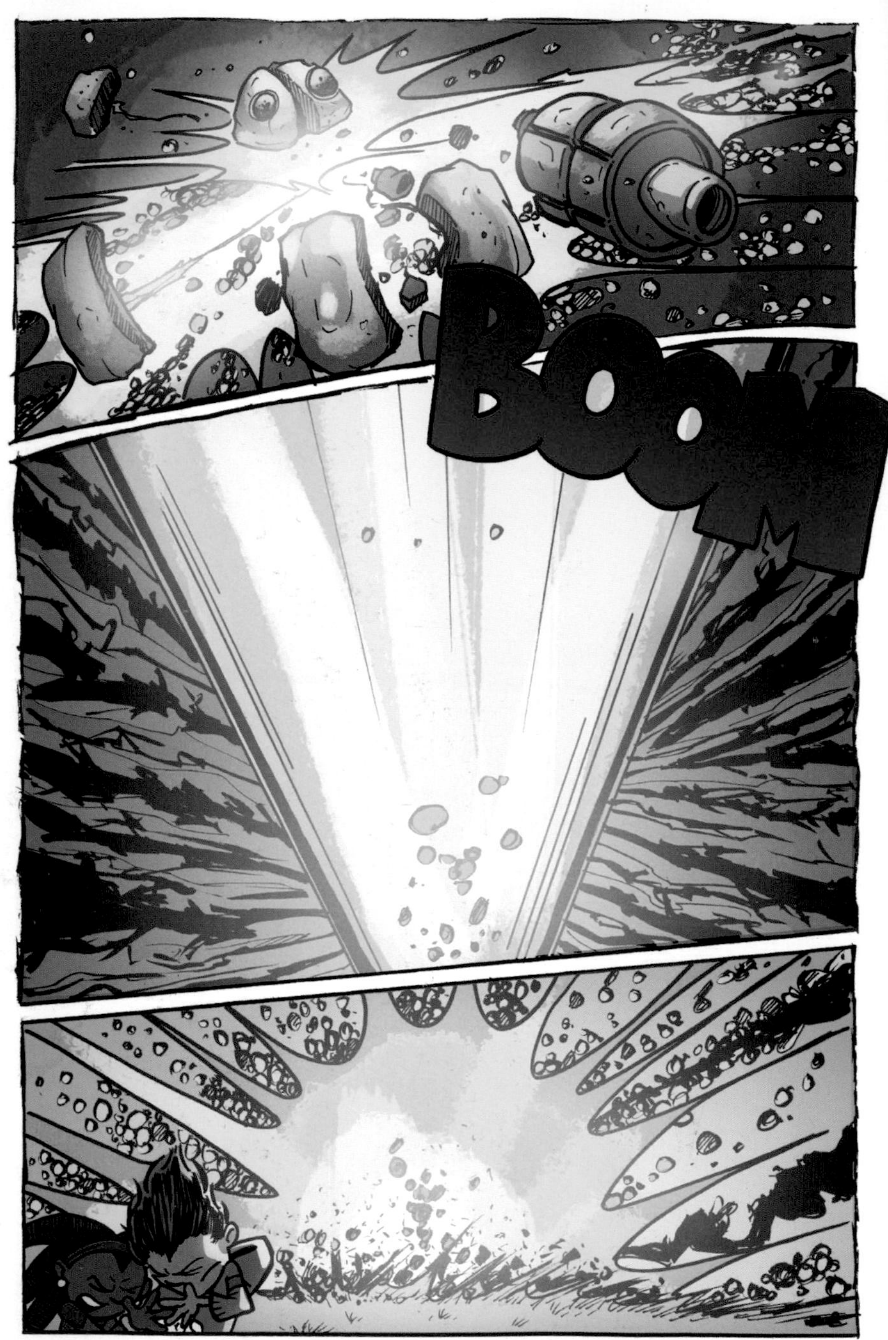
BOOM

HILO?
OW.
HEY!
YOU DID IT!
NO.
NOT EXACTLY.

SRAAAAAACCK
CROOM

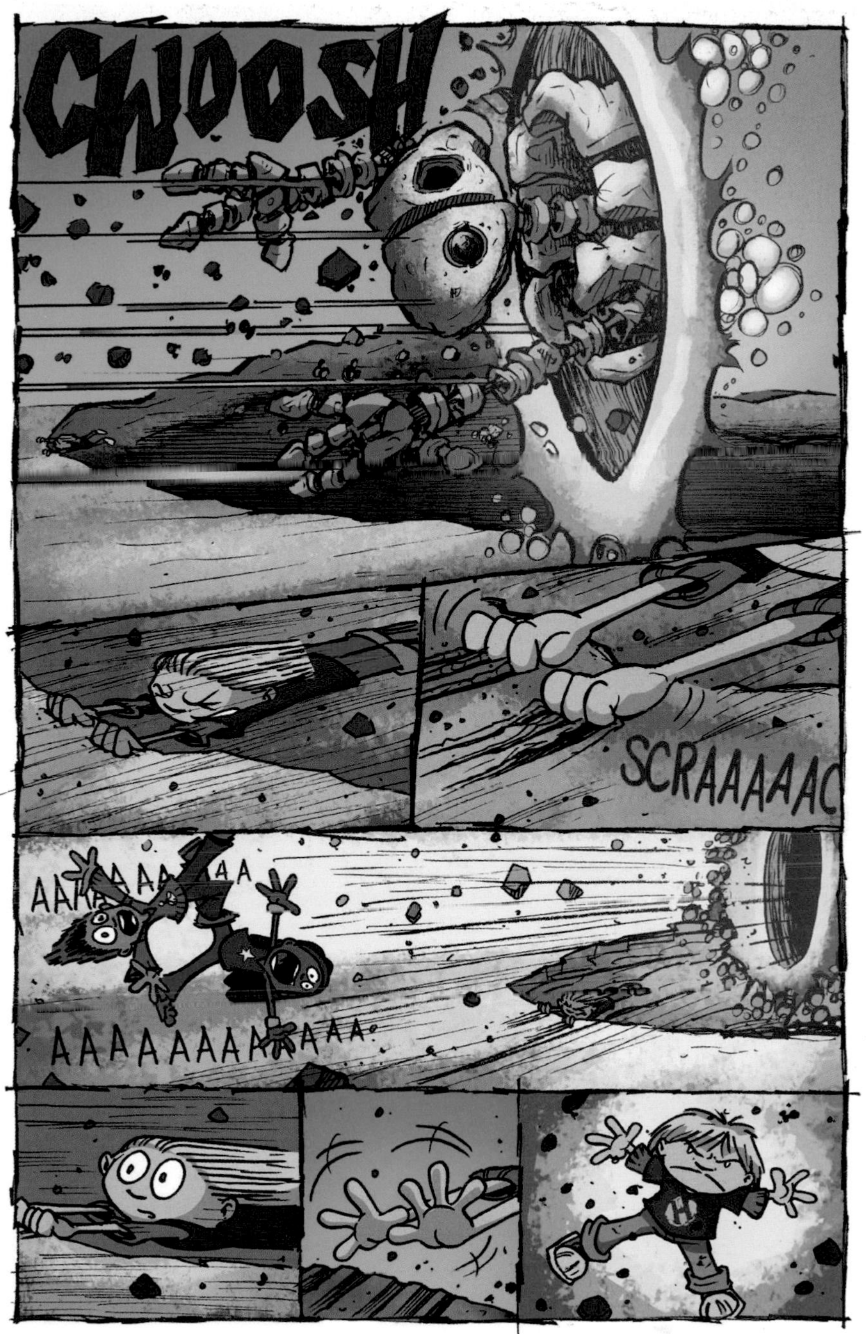
CHOOSH
SCRAAAAAC
AAAAAAAAAA
AAAAAAAAAAA

WHUMP
WHAT'S HAPPENING?!
IT'S A HOLE! A PORTAL TO TAKE ME BACK TO MY WORLD!
NO!
IT'S OKAY, D. J.! I HAVE TO GO BACK!

PLEASE! DON'T GO! I CAN HELP YOU!
YOU ALREADY HAVE HELPED ME!
YOU REMINDED ME WHO I NEED TO BE!
A BOY FELL FROM THE SKY, AND ALL YOU WANTED TO DO IS PROTECT HIM!
YOU SAVED HIM BY THROWING A ROBOT OFF A CLIFF, LEAPING DOWN A PITCH-BLACK HOLE, FIGHTING A GIANT METAL BUG WITH A STICK --
AND A WHOLE LOT MORE!
YOU'RE GOOD AT A LOT MORE THAN ONE THING!
YOU'RE BRAVE! AND YOU'D NEVER RUN AWAY! I NEED TO BE LIKE YOU!
YOU'RE OUTSTANDING, DANIEL JACKSON LIM!

TZOT
TZOT
TZOT
TZOT
TZOT
TZOT
WHUMP
WHUMP

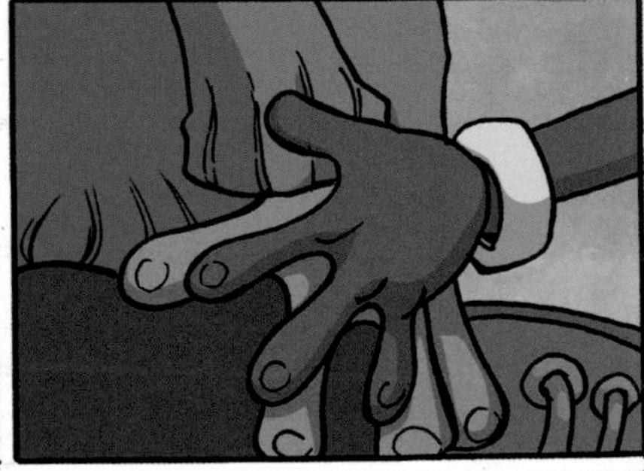

CHAPTER 9

GONE

ABBOTT

TIME

D.J.
D.J.?
HILO?!
YES.
IT'S ME.
HOW ARE YOU?

ME? HOW AM I? **ME?!** I'M OKAY!
WHERE ARE YOU?!
I DON'T KNOW.
WELL, I DON'T KNOW WHERE **MOST** OF ME IS.

WHAT?
IT'S A LITTLE WEIRD.
OPEN THE BOTTOM DRAWER OF YOUR DESK.

EW.
YEAH.
MAXIMILLION
WHAT IS IT?

MY TOE.
EW.
MAXIMILLION
I KNOW. IT'S A LITTLE WEIRD.

I WAS GOING TO LEAVE AN **EAR,** BUT THAT'S GROSS TOO AND I REALLY NEED MY EARS. BUT ANYWAY --
I HAD TO LEAVE A BIT OF ME BEHIND.

WHY?

IN CASE I NEEDED TO TALK TO YOU.

SOMETHING TERRIBLE HAS HAPPENED.

I NEED YOUR HELP.

WHAT DO I HAVE TO DO?

YOU HAVE TO GO.
NOW.
GET GINA.

IS THAT **REALLY** YOUR TOE? **EW!**
I KNOW, IT'S A LITTLE WEIRD.
HILO! WHERE DO WE NEED TO GO?!

WHERE YOU FOUND ME.
WHERE I FELL TO EARTH.

OKAY, WE'RE ALMOST THERE. I --

SKIIIIIIIIID

YOU SEE IT?
YES.

HILO ... WHAT'S GOING ON?

IT'S BAD.
I THOUGHT I COULD END THIS BY GOING BACK ... BUT IT'S JUST BEGUN.

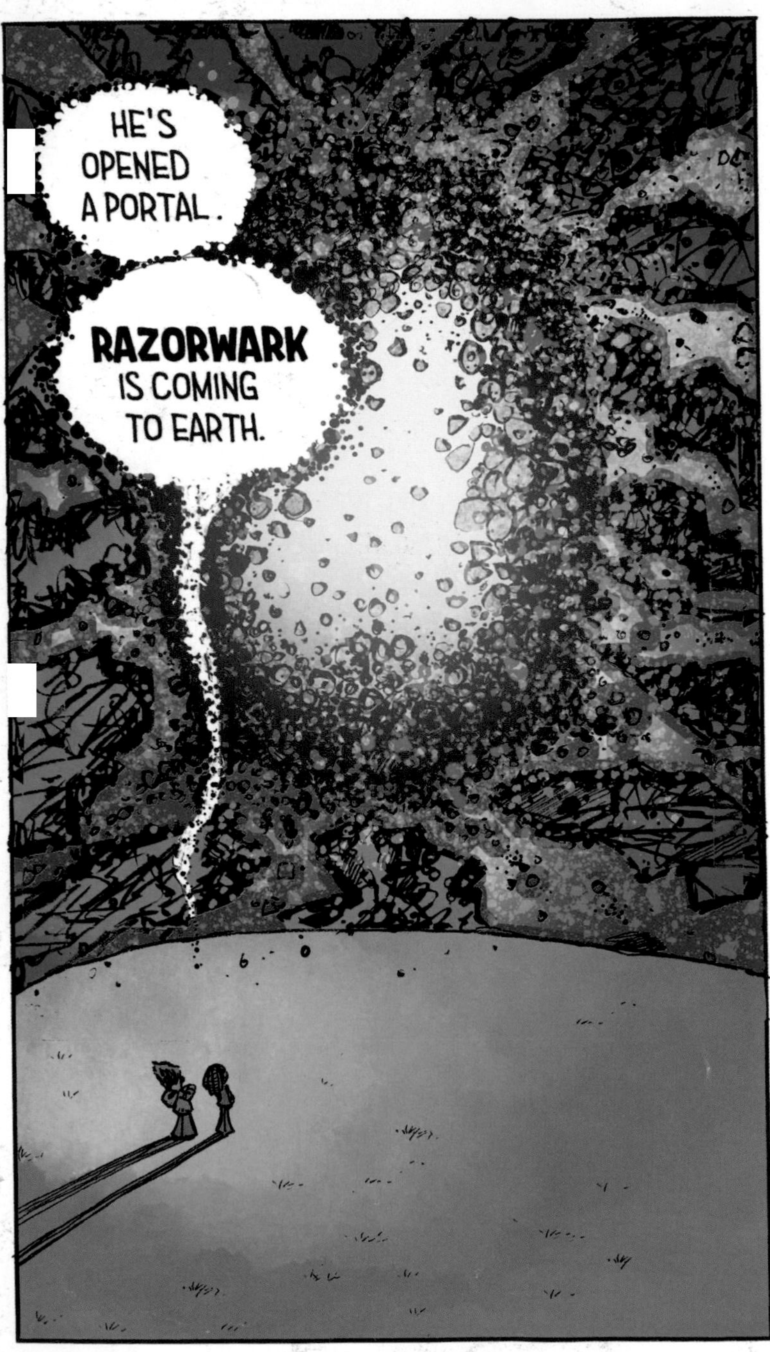
HE'S OPENED A PORTAL.
RAZORWARK IS COMING TO EARTH.

END OF BOOK ONE

DON'T MISS HILO'S SECOND AMAZING ADVENTURE

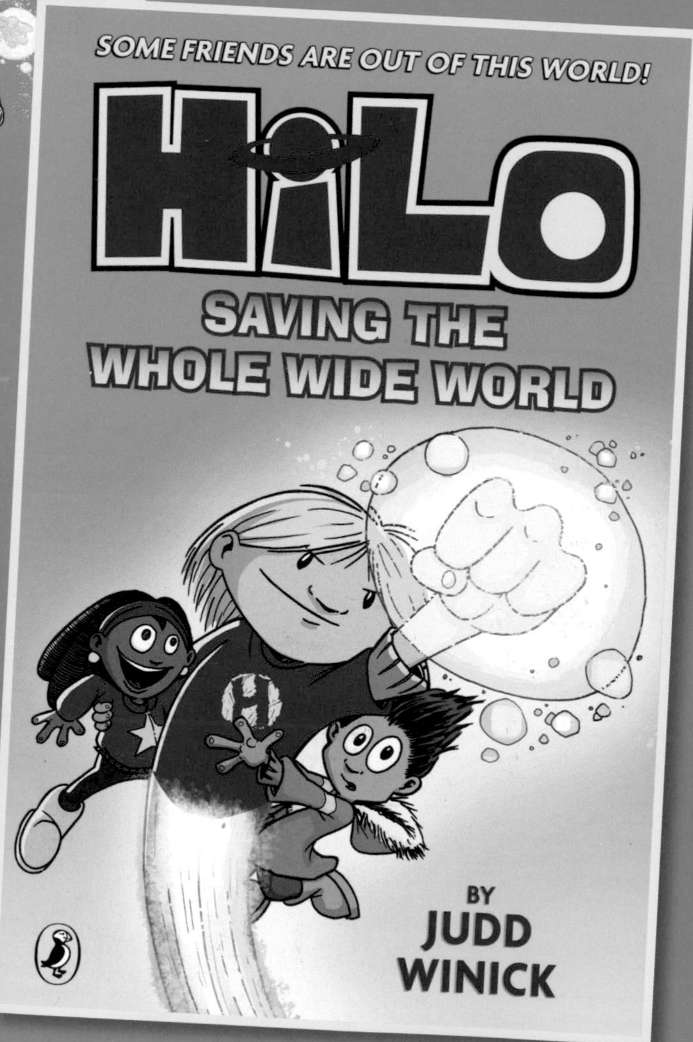

AVAILABLE NOW!

DON'T MISS HILO'S THIRD OUTSTANDING APPEARANCE

AVAILABLE NOW!

JUDD WINICK grew up on Long Island, where he spent countless hours doodling, reading **X-Men** comics and the newspaper strip **Bloom County**, and watching **Looney Tunes**. Today Judd lives in San Francisco with his wife, Pam Ling; their two kids; and their cat, Chaka. When Judd isn't collecting far more action figures and vinyl toys than a normal adult, he is a screenwriter and an award-winning cartoonist. Judd has scripted issues of bestselling comics series, including Batman, Green Lantern, Green Arrow, Justice League, and Star Wars. Judd also appeared as a cast member of MTV's **The Real World: San Francisco** and is the author of the highly acclaimed graphic novel **Pedro and Me**, about his **Real World** castmate and friend, AIDS activist Pedro Zamora. Visit Judd and Hilo online at **juddspillowfort.com**.